NORTH COAST
COLLECTED

By
Members of the
Prince Rupert Writers' Group
with special thanks to
Jean Rysstad
who acted as the Group's contact
with the publisher.

edited by Dave Speck

The Caitlin Press
Prince George, British Columbia

The Caitlin Press
P.O. Box 2387, Station B
Prince George, B.C. V2N 2S6
Canada

Caitlin Press would like to acknowledge the financial support
of the Canada Council and the British Columbia Cultural
Fund.

Cover Design by Glenn Singleton

Cover Photo by Nancy Robertson

Typeset by Denis & Muntener Advertising, Prince George

Printed in Canada

Canadian Cataloguing in Publication Data

North coast collected
Selections by members of the Prince Rupert Writers' Group,
previously published in North coast collection.

ISBN 0-920576-50-8

1. Canadian literature (English)—British Columbia—Prince
Rupert. 2. Canadian literature (English)—20th century.* I.
Speck, Dave, 1941- II. Prince Rupert Writers' Group. III.
Title: North coast collection.
PS8257.P75N67 1994   C810.8'097111   C94-910498-1
PR9198.3.P752N67 1994

PREFACE

I first visited Prince Rupert in the early seventies when I attended one of the first large-scale conferences of First Nations leaders who were working out a response to the federal government's proposal to do away with special status for aboriginal peoples. I think it's fitting that one of the first such conferences was held in Prince Rupert, as this city always celebrated its diversity. This anthology reflects the many cultures and lifestyles that add up to life in Northwest British Columbia.

I don't remember much of the conference itself, but I do remember Prince Rupert. Mist so fine, I couldn't call it rain. Pastel colored houses on trapezoid-shaped lots with wooden boardwalks leading to the streets while lawns sloped downward, to end sometimes ten feet below the road surface. Then there's the First Nation's influence. Totem poles, carvings, paintings, and finely worked silver. These were just the obvious influences.

There wasn't the grid-lock development I'd come to know in the south coastal cities. I sniffed the salty, tangy air and was transported home to growing up on B.C.'s wild coast where the ocean was the main transportation system; roads came later and didn't determine where people lived, but rather, became a link between where people had already settled. People determined settlement patterns, not the settlement pattern determining how people interacted.

I now live 800 kilometres from the nearest salt air, but I haven't forgotten Prince Rupert's siren song. And *North Coast Collected* sings that song.

It does not surprise me that out of this seemingly isolated city of 16,000 people, they are able to pull together enough "good stuff" to publish an anthology of some of B.C.'s best writing yet. It's what you would expect, once you've visited Prince Rupert.

The Prince Rupert Writer's Group began sometime in the early 1980s - no one seems really sure of the exact date, though some mention 1981 as likely. In 1985, the Group began publishing an annual collection of writings. But again, it wasn't a clear cut beginning, as the Group had published two volumes earlier. Be that as it may, they began to publish professional, competent anthologies in 1985, as one might expect out of Prince Rupert.

In true northern tradition, the Group widened its net and offered writers from all over B.C., through ads in B.C. Bookworld and the B.C. Writers Union newsletter, a chance to be published. The Group's mandate, according to Jean Rysstad, is to promote and encourage the unknown, unpublished writers of British Columbia. (Jean is one of Prince Rupert's best known writers, was main initiator of the present volume and is a contributer to this volume.)

Eight volumes of poetry, fiction and non fiction followed which commonly sold out the annual 2000 print run over the next eight years. The group approached Caitlin Press in October 1992, asking us if we would consider a "best of" anthology.

Originally, I turned The Group down saying that I wanted a wider geographical base – all of northern B.C. – not realizing the treasure trove I had in my manuscript pile. Dave Speck, who compiled, selected, and edited the works that comprise *North Coast Collected*, convinced me that Caitlin Press didn't need to look any farther afield – more than enough for a fine anthology was right under my nose. And the result is the book you hold in your hands.

Enjoy your reading.

Cynthia Wilson
Publisher

CONTENTS

Preface   V
The Pretty Little Fisherman   K. Miller   01
The Unfolding of My Regional Consciousness   B. Hermanek   03
Reality is Flat and Cool   Zoë Landale   06
Puffins and Stuff   Don Phipps   08
Joe   N. J. Kerby   10
The Broken Hand   E. W. Gant   12
Old Fred   Stewart Brinton   15
Remembering   Glenn Allen   16
Shopping for Shrimp   Dan Branch   17
Fire at the Pawn Shop   Eileen O'Brien Richards   20
The Second River   LaVerne Adams   23
Horsefaith   Allen Smith   29
Albert as Hero   Joan Skogan   30
Butter   Grace Hols   36
Ketchikan   Dina von Hahn   40
Natty Creek Garden Journal   Deanna Kawatski   41
Le Patinage Noir   Lynda Orman   48
Indefatigable in a Bottle   Iain Lawrence   49
Nanabush   George Stanley   53
On Folding a Rowboat   Sheila Peters   55
Starting School   Liz McKenna   62
Waiting for Peter   Iain Lawrence   64
An Unexpectedly Tender Document   Joan Skogan   69
Men in Stanfield Grays   Paul McCuish   70
Old Yoehta and the Young Hunter   Joan Skogan   79
Midden, Prince Rupert Harbour   Andrew Wreggitt   82
True North   Joan Skogan   84
Merger   Joanna M. Weston   89
Timber   Kenneth Campbell   90

Gwaii Haanas	Jenny Nelson	97
Josephine	N. J. Kerby	99
Burying Hugh	Marylou Fritch	106
Grounding Time	Leslie Yates	108
Lovebites	Jean Rysstad	114
Indelible	Nancy Robertson	121
The Preface Is	JoAnne Ames	123
En Boca Cerrada	Dorothy Trail Spiller	124
Petroglyph	Kenneth Campbell	131
Between the River and the Road	Dorothy Trail Spiller	132
Northerners versus Nuppies	Barrie Abbott	139
Familiar Trails	Nancy Robertson	142
Deuce	Grace Hols	146
Angels	Claudia Stewart	151
Dear Abby	Liz McKenna	153
Axeman	Marylou Fritch	155
Messing with the River Gods	Mallory Burton	159
Lottery	N. J. Kerby	163
Devilfish	Andrew Wreggitt	164
On the Boardwalk, Bamfield	Richard Mackie	166
Family Isle	Gerry Deiter	168
Married at Heritage Park	N. J. Kerby	172
The Fourth of November	Pat Barry	173
The Redeemer	Dorothy Trail Spiller	177
The Emerger	Mallory Burton	178
Lunch	E. W. Gant	181

K. Miller

Kristin Miller was born in Seattle; she has lived on the North Coast for fifteen years. Quiltmaker, boater, mental health worker, she is the author of *The Careless Quilter*.

"On the North Coast, women wait for fishermen to come back, then wait for them to leave again. In other places, they wait for truck drivers, salesmen, or soldiers."

Pull out your old chin whiskers, lady
And strap on your high heeled shoes.
Here comes your pretty little fisherman,
Home from the seven seas.

Cinch your waist real tight
And make sure you're looking good:
Here comes your pretty fisherman,
He wants to reel you in.

Put some perfume on your earlobes.
Pour the wine into the glass.
Take off those smelly fish clothes
And give him what you've got.

Give him loving, give him kisses,
Give him breakfast, hugs, and moans.
Your man has been a-fishing
And he wants it good and hot.

Don't wear your old grey bathrobe
Don't fight or bitch or rage:
Your man's come home from fishing
But he'll soon be gone again.

Right now he's into kissing
But he won't be for long
His thoughts'll turn back to fishing
And he'll sing a different song

So be his starlit mermaid.
Be his great delight.
Don't be no cold fish mama:
It's only for tonight.

THE UNFOLDING OF MY REGIONAL CONSCIOUSNESS

B. Hermanek

Bela Hermanek's life appears in this story. She likes inspiring conversation, good movies *(The Piano)*, good books *(The English Patient)*, and flamenco dancing *(Antonio Gades)*. She has lived on the B.C. Coast for many years.

Until you move to a different region, or even a different country, you are not really aware of having such a thing as regional consciousness. You can observe some immigrants adjusting, but it is not your "skin which is being put on the drum."

Born in Czechoslovakia, we all thought our country to be the heart of Europe. But sitting inside a cup, one knows little about what is going on outside the rim. In the time of Stalin's personality cult, we got used to not saying in the school what we heard at home. Everybody knew; everybody had double lives and pretended in public. Fifteen million people pretending — it was like we all went to a national acting school! Twenty long years we lived with socialism, loving it and hating it, trying to justify it to ourselves. Those years will always remain a sore spot in my heart.

In 1968 when things started to look up, I lost my country through foreign invasion. I was on holiday in Switzerland when it happened, so I stayed and lived there for the next ten years.

The Swiss people also believed they lived in the heart of Europe, but of western Europe. Land behind the Iron Curtain was *terra incognita* for them, an unknown land with savages running around. Here I was first made aware of my regional consciousness.

In Switzerland, everything was different. The beauty of the Alps and clean streets couldn't make up for the sweetness of rolling hills and the fish ponds of my homeland. I was missing the black-humoured, emotional Bohemians, with their love of food, sex, music, and beer. There was no comparison to these well dressed, safe and careful Swiss, money-conscious beyond belief. They could identify one's wealth by the family name, and the region one came from by a specific dialect because people there live in the same places for centuries. With my accent and my maiden name, Kloboucnikova, I felt like an exotic animal nobody really wanted to be too close to. When I called a dog he didn't come to me; he spoke a different language. The clouds were different; the meadows didn't smell the same. All the excellent chocolate and Swiss cheese couldn't make up for my feeling of not belonging. Home sweet home. One only appreciates it after one loses it. In Switzerland everything was already discovered and perfect. I found an adventurous Czech husband, and as quickly as possible, we were ready for a new country.

If one grows up in a cup, it is an amazing experience to drive across Canada. You drive for weeks, still in the same country. It is the space, I believe, that makes people so relaxed and friendly. Finally, we visited a friend on the Queen Charlotte Islands and decided to stay there. We went to the police station in Masset for registration. The officer couldn't believe his ears; in Canada, we were informed, people don't register. We realized how brainwashed our European background had made us.

We continued speaking Czech. Our little daughter, born in Switzerland, first learned English in a playschool run by Haida mothers and nannies on the Haida Indian Reserve. After two years there, she spoke their English and also learned some Haida dancing.

In the meantime, we opened a Bohemian restaurant, a little bit of our homeland, where people might share good food and good times. We still felt as Europeans. During our first six years, we hadn't offered any fast food, hadn't even owned a deep frier. But when the Chinese bought a restaurant in town, we learned quickly the rules of competition in capitalism. Our regional identity began to change again.

The Charlottes grew on us unavoidably: the beautiful fairytale-like rain forest, the beaches, the tides, the people. The annual Community Christmas Concert is like a big family gathering; everybody knows everybody and has a great time.

When the Haida protested on Lyell Island a few years ago, we were given nationwide T.V. coverage. Finally Canadians learned that the Queen Charlotte Islands are part of British Columbia! (Still, when we order supplies from Vancouver, they usually reply, "We deliver only in B.C.")
Now the tourists are arriving in bigger groups and we locals experience a new feeling of regional consciousness. How will the visitors perceive our Islands? Do we want them here?

After the 1990 Velvet Revolution in Czechoslovakia, I could finally return "home," twenty-two years later. Travelling with my two children, born in Masset, who understood my mother tongue but did not speak it, I was forced to suppress all those overwhelming emotions. For six weeks I couldn't wear any make-up because I cried on every corner.

Prague was still amazingly majestic: the old churches, towers, cobblestones. But it stunk and it was crowded and malfunctioning. Every single thing was devastated; people were discouraged. When I spoke of stunningly clean salty air, of water I can drink from every creek I happened to walk by, of our house we never lock — they looked at me with disbelief and envy. It felt good to lose some illusions about Europe.

My regional consciousness is mixed up, as one can see. I usually try to sing the Canadian national anthem with full voice, and often am bewildered when I see how many students in the school don't know the words, couldn't care less, or choose not to sing at all. As children back in Czechoslovakia, we didn't have the freedom to choose. We were drilled to be patriots. Ironically our national anthem's title was: "Where is My Home, Where is My Home?"

Lately, I have found the answer. The North Coast is my home.

Zoë Landale

Zoë Landale fished commercially off the North Coast for seven years. Landale's work has appeared in many magazines, twenty anthologies, and her third book is forthcoming from Cacanadadada Press. She lives with her family in Ladner, BC.

"Reality is Flat and Cool" came from a desire to be back on the water again.

I want to be stitched back
to the slow unfurl
of coast
like a dropped thread
welcomed home.

To welcome fathoms of water,
half-substantial, light-danced
and horizontal, horizontal in all directions
against roots
of sky-flung coast ranges

Blue, etched against light;
thrown rock.
Beyond islands, green   of near trees,
jut   of headlands,
passages open, obediant to charts

Open, and your engine noisily
vibrates vision from one misty point
to the next,
your steer compass courses, wheel
varnish-slick to fingers

Carry islands in your eyes
wind-distorted evergreens
degrees   of course,
cool slide-past
of drying rocks.

The coast unreels through 360 degrees,
reality is flat and cool, goes down dark
for fathoms.
With each revolution of the propeller
wake   tosses white stitches ashore.

Don Phipps

Born in Powell River, Don Phipps moved to Prince Rupert where he worked on seiners and trollers until 1988. "The industry has turned into nothing more than an over-regulated mess that makes us all so competitive that the fun and comradeship has gone right out of it." He lives with his family in Telkwa, BC.

"Puffins and Stuff," is based on Phipps' experiences at sea.

I don't know what I'm doing here in the middle of Hecate Strait. I hate it here. Every time I decide to troll, it blows thirty knots from the southeast or the southwest. And this time is no different.

Fishing dried up on the top end of the Queen Charlotte Islands where I normally fish, so I ran down here to the Shell Ground, hoping for better things. But waking up this morning to everything smashing and crashing, barely able to gain my footing to get dressed and get up to the galley to put the coffee on, I just knew it was going to be one of those days.

By the time the coffee's ready it's almost daylight, time to haul the anchor and start fishing. All the time I'm saying to myself, "If it's fishy enough I'll stay, but if I don't catch enough to satisfy myself, I'll move on."

Once the gear's in the water and I've started a tack, it doesn't seem so bad. There's plenty of bird life and the odd fish is climbing on. After a couple of hours of this, though, the weather is deteriorating and the handful of boats that were here this morning have disappeared. After counting the fish in the checkers, I decide it's time for a move. I haul the gear aboard and start running due south, heading for Logan Inlet on the east coast of the Charlottes.

It seems like a long haul to reach the lee of the land, with weather conditions worsening, but once I'm into Logan Inlet it's all inside travelling. Passing Tanu Island I conjure up images of what it must have been like when the Haida people had settlements scattered all over the Charlottes. Before long I'm through the pass and into Darwin Sound, on a southeast heading. Soon I can tell I'm approaching Juan Perez Sound. I can feel the familiar ocean swell under the boat again.

By now it's getting pretty late in the evening, and I figure that by the time I get to Section Cove, it'll be too late to do any fishing so I might as well anchor up and get a good night's sleep. Then I'll be ready to give 'er hell tomorrow.

With the anchor set, shutting down the engine is like someone lifting a great load off my shoulders. Then I start to realize how tired I really am, so it's a quick supper and into the bunk.

Four and a half hours later, the alarm shoves me into a new day. Before I can think clearly, I'm dressed, have the coffee on, and the anchor up. I can see it's going to be a fine day and I don't want to miss the sunrise, so in the half dark I start out for Scudder Point.

Through the narrow pass between Burnaby Island and Huxley Island I watch for the tell-tale signs of the dark shadow on the water that indicate hidden rocks on the port side. Then I head toward Alder Island, watching for the rock on the starboard side. Through the narrow gap between Alder Island and Burnaby Island, then it's out toward Saw Reef.

The sky is brightening more by the minute and I see a pink-orange glow on the unbroken horizon to the northeast. I quickly put the gear in the water, get positioned on the tack, and pour myself a cup of coffee, then thrill to the beauty of the sunrise.

Once the sun is fully up, I start to pay attention to what I'm doing. I'm getting out closer to the spot now and I see a couple of lines going. I pick off a couple of cohos. Then I see what I'm looking for — birds! Thousands of them! Eagles and seagulls and puffins and stuff, all working in a feeding frenzy.

All my lines are going and soon the checkers and decks are running red with coho blood. I know, I really know, this is going to be a day to remember.

Somehow the previous day of uncertainty, disappointment, and fatigue has slipped away. But I also know that when I anchor up tonight, I'll be wondering how long today's type of fishing will last. How soon will I be forced to leave here and reluctantly head back out into the much-dreaded Hecate Strait?

But for now, this day is all I ask.

N. J. Kerby

Norma Kerby is a long-time northwest B.C. resident who receives her inspiration for her character poems from the area and its residents. She is an instructor at Northwest Community College in Terrace, B.C. Her poetry has been published in a variety of journals.

Joe   on his bicycle   through the summer heat haze
        Mirage   above the highway   he floats
Joe   hardhat   lunchbox
At 3:10 p.m. precise another shift change and Joe on his bicycle
On the hill on the highway a ghost in the heat waves
                        Pedalling on air.

Sawmill town   the young bucks drive hot cars
        even the guys on the clean-up crew have Eldorados
But Joe   sweat dripping from his nose
Riding the rusty grinding bicycle he bought from old man Finter
            half a fender   no padding on the seat
                                    he walked in winter
        day-old bread for lunch   rotten bananas from the
                                            specials bin
Say, Joe, whatthehell are you doing with all your money?
Banter in the coffee room   Who, Me? Oh, yeah, Me. Got
Lotsa   kids to feed back in Italy   country villa
        big cheese in Milano when I go back
    next year,
                            'nother son
                Me? They think I'm king here in Canada.

Joe   on his bicycle   through the ground-hugging
        burner smoke
                                    late for work

There wasn't much of Joe
         to send to the old country
After the   lumber truck
       hit him.
And the boys at the mill don't watch the hill on the highway
      anymore
Mirages have a funny way of looking like
        a man on a bicycle   floating in air.

E. W. Gant

Eric Gant owns a dive fishing company specializing in harvesting gourmet foods from the sea. As well he is president of a consortium of aquaculture companies working to change dive fisheries from hunting to ranching the sea.

"The Broken Hand" was written when he was a bushman.

Jimmy and I moved along the frozen surface of the lake in silence. Three miles behind us, out near the centre of the lake, sat a diamond drill tripod coated with ice. On shore ahead of us were two dingy tents half hidden in a lonely growth of spruce. The snow covered, grey stubbled hills looming up behind the tents made us look like two black bugs as we walked off the white belly of the lake.

Jimmy, walking ahead of me, slipped on the narrow packed trail and floundered hip deep into the soft snow by the side. I squatted on the trail to wait, and loosened my parka to let the cold bite at my throat and chest, cooling me away from the beginnings of a light sweat.

An hour before, back at the drill, Jimmy had gotten his hand caught side-ways between a tightening chain and the hind leg of the tripod. Now his freshly broken hand, the cold, and the hour long walk back to camp were making him clumsy.

When he was on the path again, he pushed his hood back from his scowling face and went down on one knee beside me, stuffing his broken hand back into the pocket of his parka. Our breath steamed into the forty-below air as we looked out at the silent hills surrounding the lake. A mile away, a wolf loped with lowered head across the mouth of a bay and disappeared back into the bush. We rested for a few moments in the stillness until the cold started to steal through our clothing. Then we moved on towards the tents.

They were good tents for wintering in — big and square and tall enough for a six-foot-four man like myself to stand in without stooping. Each had a canvas snow apron over the top, a plywood floor, and a stove. Chunks of dried muskeg were banked along the outside of the canvas walls to help block out the wind. A woman lived in the first tent, serving us satisfying meals of meat dripping with the hot fat craved by men who live in the cold. The second tent, connected to the first by a path, was where we slept. As we moved off the edge of the lake, Jimmy slipped again.

When he fell, he twisted his body to keep from falling on his hand and landed with his face in the snow. He spit out a curse word in Cree, kicking back at the snow to get even. The sound of his voice carried to the tents, but there was no response.

"The cook must be asleep," I said.

We moved up the path to the second tent and went in. The dimness inside relieved the eyes after the snow-hard brightness of the lake. In each corner of the tent there was a bunk with an eiderdown sleeping bag rolled up at its foot. Jimmy sat down slowly on his bunk without removing his parka. I tramped the snow off my boots and went over to the stove in the centre. Opening the top lid, I stacked dry wood on top of the slowly burning green.

Using his teeth, Jimmy pulled the mitt off his good hand, then eased his broken one into the open. I looked over at it as I shucked my parka. The fingers appeared unbroken but the hand itself was bent into only half its proper width and two broken bones poked their jagged ends up against the skin on the back.

I had a bottle of Canadian Club stashed in my duffel bag. I dug it out, cracked the seal, and brought it over to him. He took a small swallow, waited for it to settle, then took two more, each longer than the one before. He drank well for a seventeen-year-old. I checked the fire to see that it was catching and then sat down on my bunk. Jimmy stared sadly at the far wall, drinking methodically.

"When the foreman comes in tonight," I said, "he'll radio the company and they'll send out the plane in the morning to fly you to town."

"No," he said. "I can't go to town. The company will fire me."

"Well sure," I shrugged. "They usually do that to keep their compensation rates down. But that means nothing. They'll pay your hospital bills and hire you back as soon as you're better. They did that to me once when I got gangrene from an axe cut."

"Not me," he said.

"Why not? You're a good worker like I am."

"But you are white," he said, embarrassed that a boy should have to tell a man of such things. He took another drink. His throat clenched on the last swallow as it tried to come back up. The fire in the tin stove hissed and cracked in the silence as the green wood passed its heat to the dry air.

Jimmy carefully set the half-empty bottle onto the floor. Then he pried gently at his hand. He wanted to flatten it so he could go back to work the next day, but I could see that he couldn't will himself past the pain. He gave it up and sat staring at the floor. Then he got down on his knees, placed his broken hand on the floor and said, "Step on it."

I looked at his lowered head for a moment then got up from my bunk and walked slowly over to stand in front of him. I placed the heel of my boot on the floor in front of his fingers and lowered the sole onto his hand. The cramped flesh slowly gave under the pressure and flattened onto the floor. Jimmy's head sagged. I kept the hand pinned for several seconds to give the muscles a chance to get used to being back in position.

A low whine started deep in his throat and built into an agonizing cry but he did not try to move his hand until I released the pressure. He hunched back cradling his hand, bowing backwards and forwards in the dimness of the tent until the worst of the pain had passed. Then he rolled back onto his bunk, faced into the wall and closed his eyes. His body shivered in spasms as I loosened the lacings on his boots and covered him with his eiderdown.

I picked up the half-full bottle and went to sit on my bunk. I don't know how long I watched him, but the tent was starting to darken before I finally took a long swallow from the bottle and laid down to sleep.

OLD FRED

Stewart Brinton

Stewart Brinton lived in Prince Rupert for over 10 years. He has had articles published in *Alaska Magazine* and *Beautiful British Columbia*. His interests include writing and music.

On Remembrance Day, I always think of Old Fred. His full name was Fred Lowther. I always called him "Old Fred." He died a few years ago, in his eighties, a veteran of World War I. He hated Remembrance Day. He'd shut himself in his cabin, wouldn't even turn on his radio. He despised the idea of rosy-cheeked school girls placing wreaths on graves while silver-tongued politicians recited poems about courage and honor, freedom and liberty.

Fred had no patience with the celebrators of war. He'd been in all the major Canadian battles of World War I — Ypres, Sommes, Vimy Ridge. Of the fifteen young and robust enlistees from the coastal community of Texada Island, Fred was the only one who returned home — the sole survivor.

For Fred, survival was more of a curse than a blessing. He'd lost all his boyhood friends in the war. It changed him. He never kept his uniform or his medals — he burned them. Embittered, he never married, never had children.

He became a postal clerk, dutifully delivering the mail, and spent the rest of his life trying to forget a war he could not forget.

After the Armistice of 1918, Texada Island, like communities all over Canada, erected a cement cenotaph as a war memorial. Attached to it was a brass plaque inscribed with the motto "Lest We Forget." Over the decades the monument decayed.

Deer hunters took potshots at it. Teenagers defaced it with graffiti. The iron bolts fastening the plaque rusted away, and the plaque with its inscription, "Lest We Forget" dropped unceremoniously to the ground. That's what enraged old Fred; the irony of "Lest We Forget." Because everyone had forgotten — except the front line veterans.

That's why Remembrance Day is the day when I always think of Old Fred. It's the day we remember to forget the real horror of war. It's a macabre celebration, with everyone wearing bright red poppies pinned to their lapels — like little bullet wounds. Old Fred once told me that Remembrance Day was the saddest day of the year. It was the day he could hear the screaming of wounded horses. That was the most horrible thing he'd experienced . . . the screaming of wounded horses.

Glenn Allen

Glenn Allen was born near Shelburne, Nova Scotia. He lived in Prince Rupert for over 10 years. His recent projects include producing eleven original songs with Vancouver producer Larry Volen.

"Remembering" was written in response to CBC Radio's Peter Gzowski's challenge to three of his *Morningside* show poet guests to write a poem within a twenty- minute time limit.

Oh I remember when I was a boy
The winters were made for one reason:
Racing down the hill behind our home
Riding my old brown toboggan.

Play became work as I grew older
The winters were made for one reason:
Trudging out to the bush, horses in hand
For dad and I to go logging.

Where I live today, winters are made
Without any snow for toboggans:
Gingerly, I ease out my front door
To work at the play called jogging.

I don't mind the jogging,
I enjoyed the logging —
But what I would give to again be that boy
Swooshing down the hill on that old brown toboggan.

Dan Branch

Dan Branch lives in Ketchikan, Alaska where he squeezes humour and poetry out of his IBM clone. His awards include a University of Alaska Southeast Award for poetry. Dan writes a column for the *Alaska Bar Rag*.

His writing, including "Shopping for Shrimp," is based on experiences on the North Coast.

Before I came to Alaska, I had blithely assumed that if, for example, you wanted bread, then you would go to a bakery. It was also a pretty safe bet that you could find shoes in a shoe store. But it took Maggie to set me straight about shopping in Ketchikan.

She stopped me at the door of our local fish market the other day. "I hope you are not here to buy shrimp," she said, "for that would be a big mistake." I expected a warning about tainted product or the danger of consuming high cholesterol shellfish. Instead, Maggie gave me a lesson in economics.

"Only a Ketchikan rookie," she told me, "would buy shrimp at the fish market. Smart people get their big spotted shrimp at the Potlatch Bar. I buy the smaller striped ones at the local newspaper office."

I was having a hard time believing my friend, so I asked with a hint of sarcasm if she bought her fruit at the public utility office. She explained with great patience that, "as everybody knows, one buys fruit at the Wolf Point Scenic Turnout."

"Oh sure," I told her, "and you probably get your crabs there too."

"No," she said, "I get them at the supermarket."

When I denied ever seeing live crabs for sale there, she told me to look in the parking lot.

After growing weary of her effort to educate the fiscally impaired, Maggie left the store. I headed for the counter to make a purchase and found Julie looking over the inventory. When I told her about Maggie's unusual sources for food, Julie nodded wisely and agreed that things seem to work out that way in Ketchikan. "You have to take your wild meat where you can find it," she said. "Sometimes it turns up in strange places." I asked for an explanation. She told me a fish story.

Last week, her husband Mike and a friend took his boat over to Bostwick Bay to troll for winter king salmon. They are elusive fish, so the men planted several crab pots to increase their chances of bringing home some food. With the pots in place, Mike and his partner set out the fishing gear. After baiting their double hooks with herring, they dropped the setups over the side and ran out some line. Heavy down-rigger weights were used to ensure that the herring would dart about at the depth of forty feet.

With the lines out, Mike adjusted the throttle of the trolling motor, and the men settled in for some coffee and conversation. Half way through his second cup, Mike's pole bent over double. Mike's partner killed the outboard and reeled in his line to clear the deck for landing a very large fish. The salmon didn't run with the line or dive for the bottom. Instead, it strangely zigzagged left, then right. Mike didn't think much about this zigzag at the time. He was too busy cranking in his fish.

He brought the brute closer to the boat by carefully raising the rod tip above his head and then dipping it slowly to the water's surface as he reeled in line. When only twenty feet of monofilament were left in the water, Mike heard his prey. The beast broke the water's surface and let out a very loud quack.

Looking at the source of that very un-fish-like sound, Mike saw the light and dark feathers of a merganser at the end of his line. After a brief time on the surface, the duck dove back into the waters of Bostwick Bay. Mike overcame his foe's efforts to escape and brought the merganser to the side of the boat where his friend secured it with the net.

The bird had taken the herring cleanly and Mike's hook was lodged in its bill. Since duck season had closed a couple of months ago and Mike didn't like merganser meat anyway, he released the bird. It floated about on the surface of the bay for a while before flying to quieter waters. The men pulled their nearly full crab pots and returned home.

Her story over, Julie purchased a tee-shirt from the seafood salesman and left the store. That is when I finally figured it out. In Ketchikan, you buy underwear at the fish store, fruit and crabs in parking areas, and shrimp from the Potlatch Bar. The same Ketchikan warp must also affect the harvest of the waterfowl. I wasted a lot of time last season hunting with a shotgun and decoys. Next fall, I'll just troll for ducks with Mike.

I left the store then, intent on using my new knowledge to get the main course for dinner. I hit the Potlatch Bar, a newspaper office, and the women's clinic searching for cheap crustaceans. The clinic sent me away shrimpless but not before I picked up a birth control pamphlet entitled, "Vasectomy — the playground's still there." There were no shrimp at the newspaper office either, so I headed for the Potlatch. They were out too, so I ordered a beer, read the vasectomy pamphlet and then returned to the fish market. They were kind enough to place my shrimp in a plain brown wrapper.

Eileen O'Brien Richards

Eileen O'Brien Richards was originally from Swansea, Wales. She lived in Prince Rupert for over 16 years. "Fire at the Pawn Shop" was included in Ms Richards's book *Where Have All the People Gone*. Ms. Richards is now deceased.

We sat on Kilvey Hill waiting for Dad to come home from work. He was only home at weekends; the rest of the week, he worked in Cardiff on the dredgers. So weekends were special 'cause Dad came home. We were nine children and money was very scarce in our house, but Dad always gave us a three-penny bit for pocket money — or three-penny joys, as he called them.

"There's Dad! Look, I can see him!" shouted my sister Eileen.

We all waved madly to him, and ran down over the hill to meet him. Because I was the eldest boy, I was allowed to carry his case. We swarmed all over him. We loved him so much we could have eaten him. He always had time for us.

We rushed into the house, shouting, "Mam, our Dad's home."

She came hurrying out, and gave him a big hug. "Tired, love? Want a cup of tea?"

"Yes please; that hill gets steeper every Friday," answered Dad.

My dad was Liverpool Irish. He had a lovely accent. Mam was Welsh.

"Your tea's ready, Joseph. Sit down and I'll bring it in. It's fish and chips and apple pie."

"Before I eat, let's thank the Good Lord. He blessed me this week; I got a lot of overtime. There you are, love. Put some of it away for our trip to Liverpool."

Mam took the money and counted it. Out of the corner of her eye, she beckoned me out of the kitchen.

"Come here, son. Run down to Mendlesson, the pawn shop. Here's the tickets and the money, and get your father's best suit, shirt, and flannel drawers out of pawn."

"Okay, Mam, I'll run as fast as I can, and I'll be back before Dad's finished his dinner."

Dad had no idea Mam pawned his best clothes every Monday. He left for Cardiff at seven a.m., and by nine-thirty, his clothes were packed up and on the pawn shop shelves. Mam had to do that to put extra food on the table.

I hated going to the pawn shop; I used to hang about for ages in case I saw anyone I knew. Everyone knew Mendlesson's brown paper parcels, and I always took another shopping bag to put them in. As I got near the pawn shop, I saw Leah, one of the girls in my class. She caught me by the arm. "I know where you're going, Bob. To the pawn to get your father's clothes."

"Shut your gob, Leah, or I'll shut it for you. At least my father's got a suit to pawn."

That soon shut her up. Everyone knew how scruffy her dad was. I shook off her hand and ran on my way. Suddenly, I could smell smoke. As I rounded the corner onto Fabian's Way, I saw people everywhere, and fire engines. Firemen were training hoses on the burning pawn shop. A fireman with a big hatchet in his belt caught hold of me.

"Can't go near there, son. It's dangerous."

I looked at the crowd standing back, watching. I spotted Mr. Mendlesson.

I tugged at his sleeve. "Mr. Mendlesson, Mr. Mendlesson, it's me, Bob. Mam's sent me down to get my dad's suit out of pawn."

"Yes, Bob, I know you, but they can't save the pawn shop, let alone your father's best suit. Tell your mother to keep the ticket. She can put in a claim. Everything is well insured."

"Yes, but my dad's home and he'll want his best suit and drawers, won't he? I can't go back home without them," I told him.

"Move on, now. There's a good boy. Go away. Never mind your father's drawers," a fireman told me.

I went slowly back up Morris Lane and sat on the hill by Farmer Gray's. I started to cry. How would Mam manage without the pawn shop? And what about Dad's clothes? All hell would be let loose if Dad found his clothes had burned in the pawn shop.

A soft voice asked, "Now, young Bob, it can't be that bad. What are you crying for?"

It was my Sunday School teacher, Mrs. Evans.

"Oh, Mrs. Evans, it's terrible. My father's best suit and his flannel shirt, all burned up in the pawn shop fire," I told her through my tears.

She was very religious, was Mrs. Evans, but they had good trips in the Sunday School, and lovely Whitsun teas. She said very quietly, "Shut your eyes, Bob, and let us pray."

"Dear Lord, thank you for saving Mr. Mendlesson from death in the pawn shop. Soften Bob's father's heart. Let him not be angry about his clothes, oh Lord. But most of all, dear lord, we thank you that Bob's father is not inside his Welsh flannel drawers and his best suit. It could have been worse couldn't it, Lord? Yes, Bob's father could have been wearing them. Amen."

"There, do you feel better now, Bob?" she said with a twinkle in her eye.

I burst out laughing. She joined in. Looking at it that way, it could have been worse.

LaVerne Adams

A former North Coast resident, LaVerne Adams now lives in Chilliwack, B.C. where she coordinates UBC's Native Indian Teacher Education Program. Her works include the playscript *Medicine* (UCFV Press) and recent poetry collection *Birds Singing, Early and Late*. She was inspired to write "The Second River" by a student who was seriously ill.

"Who, me? Afraid of dying?" you titter. "Everybody has to die, don't they?" You wedge your fork through the slab of deep apple pie with the confidence of someone alive. You shut the door on death. The oven door, the closet door, the office door, the refrigerator door. All shut(tered), blinded, closed. Your molars mash the soft apples, and when you smile, there is a piece of crust stuck between your front teeth.

"I know she thinks she's by a river," you say, speaking of your mother who is delirious and dying in the hospital. "She's by a river and doesn't know how to cross. She talks about it in our native language; she knows she's dying. But the doctors don't understand that when it's time, you have to let a person die. They keep looking for new veins to put their needles in."

After the second radiation treatment for your own cancer, you are flattened by grief and nausea. In the late afternoon when you awaken and walk through the shadows of this waning February, across lemon-coloured grass layered with fog, you think about ghosts and try to remember the way of your people, the things you grew up knowing: how to ease a passing, how to guide your mother across her river. But it doesn't happen; you can't remember. You have no power after all and think that you must phone your uncle back on the Reserve to ask him what to do. When he answers, he is drunk and doesn't recognize your voice.

Now, little one
the salmon
are gone
the trees
have been cut down

and my grandchildren
do not know
who they are

In the night, beside your man, you waken with the words half-formed on your tongue and the anguish ready to leap out of your mouth. But you stifle the cry. The children are in the next room. They might hear and be frightened. Turn over, pull up the covers, nestle into his warm back. (Gentle, quiet. Don't waken him.) He seems afraid these days, even though he knows your cancer is not contagious. You have known him too long not to sense his fear and you cannot comfort him, cannot reassure him, because you wonder too.

"What if? What if. . . ?" You take advantage of the fact that he is asleep, and lie close beside the length of him until morning.

Today, as you walk home from the college, there is a tight lump knotting up, hard and painful, inside your stomach. It has nothing to do with the cancer. You know this feeling from a long way back, and see yourself, that shy, skinny Indian kid sitting in the Grade One class. The teacher's voice was so loud. You had never heard anyone talk that way before, except once or twice when your dad or one of your uncles had too much beer. You knew the teacher did not approve of you, thought you were stupid because you could not answer, could not speak in the circle when it was time to share. Today, it was almost the same, even though you are twenty-six and thought all that was forgotten.

The professor — that middle-class, middle-aged, middle-of-the-road man from the university — has what you want, and dangles it in front of you. You jump and jump, but cannot quite reach it, cannot say the right thing in the right way, cannot frame the answer to his question. When you look into his hard blue eyes, you know what he is thinking, for he said after class, in a way he thought was kindly, that you had to brush up on your general knowledge of the world. You should have known it was a mistake to ask him where the West Indies are.

When you cry, you are not sure of the reason. Is it because of your physical pain, your approaching death? Is it for your mother? Your husband and children? You sob into a towel in the bathroom so they will not hear, and think it doesn't matter anyway.

Grandfather
Speak louder!
the world is making too much noise
I cannot hear
for the traffic
is too loud
and this city
closes off my breath
like a cork
in a bottle

The children have begun to notice your illness and you know you cannot postpone much longer the telling, the sitting them down and saying the words. But it is your job to do that. Isn't that how you were raised? Indian kids know about death. You remember funerals on the Reserve (there were so many), and how your people bury their dead, not leaving them in a box alone at the graveside, as if that's where they would stay, heaped with flowers, sweet-smelling and beautiful. No. You remember staying to see the box lowered into the earth, and the people each throwing a handful or shovelful of dirt down into the grave. It is the right way to say goodbye, and you will do this for your mother when the time comes, as your children will do for you.

The anger is unexpected and sneaks up on you, like a mean trick played by Raven or Coyote. You try to ignore it, to reason it away, but it burns in your belly. You yell at the kids and watch their smooth young faces crumple with pain. And you flare up at you husband. They all avoid you when you pull dishes and pots from the kitchen cupboard and scour everything with hot water and Mr. Clean. Afterwards, slumped over the table, you think it smells like a hospital in there.

When you take the roots
of a cedar tree
to make a basket
or catch a salmon
from the river
you should thank the spirit of the river
of the tree
tell them you are grateful
for their gifts
it is never right
to just take what you need
without acknowledgement
without respect

The yellow cardigan you wore the other day would have covered the bruises on your arms if you hadn't forgotten and taken it off. You know people noticed: large, plum-coloured discs on your brown skin. "He beat me up," you said. "Came home after a few drinks and beat me up. He never hit me before. This was the first time."

You know why, of course. He is angry, too, filled with rage he doesn't understand. You remember his dark, frightened eyes as he hit you with hands that up to now had shown you love. You escaped behind the only door that locks and crouched on the edge of the bathtub until he stopped pounding on the door.

You sit beside your mother's bed and watch her chest rise and fall with rapid, shallow breaths. There are so any tubes: her arms, her nose, her mouth connected to these plastic arteries. The doctor said she was not aware of anything now, didn't feel pain. But you know better. She is still looking for a way to cross that river, to get to the other side where her friends, relatives, and children are waiting for her.

It is two a.m. and you fight sleep in spite of the headache and the pain in your body. You wish you could stretch out beside your mother and close your eyes, like you used to when you were little.

You promised the doctor you would get more rest. Once again, the radiation treatment has made you ill. It occurs to you that what is being irradiated, burned away, is not the cancer, but your spirit. You no longer feel angry, do not have the strength to fight. The disease is creeping up on you now, choking you like some forest vines choke young sprigs and saplings. The illness is stronger than you. You know it will win.

If you really want to learn
about human nature
watch the animals
in the forest
remember when birds fly
and how they know the time
to seek shelter
look at the deer
down by the river
see
how the smallest and weakest
survive despite their enemies
most of the time

At your mother's funeral, you close your eyes and see the bright water of her river. The spring sun is warm on your face, and you think of the crocuses blooming behind your rented townhouse. You meant to ask your mother if there is a name for them in your language. Now it is too late.

Your aunt and uncle have come to visit, a long way from the Reserve, but they have done it for two important reasons: it is good to visit relations in the spring when the weather is fair again, and also because they know you are dying. They do not, as others might, sit and actually talk about it, but Auntie takes you into the kitchen where she has set two sealer jars of dark liquid on the counter. Indian medicine. "It will not cure you," she says in a matter-of-fact way, "but it will help the pain."

You understand. The pain is very bad now, and you are grateful. There is no need to thank her aloud, to discuss dosages or side effects, as you might do with white doctors and white medicine. You take one of the jars and a cup to your bedroom. As you fall asleep, you hear sounds of your language being spoken, as your aunt and uncle tell about the success of last winter's traplines.

And then you dream about a river.

It is time, grandchild,
to join the sacred circle
to dance one last time
around the fire
to look in those
four directions
and accept
what you do not understand
Look!
Here is the eagle feather
you have earned
and soft white moccasins
to walk in

Allen Smith

Allen Smith has worked throughout northern B.C. He has published over 100 selections of poetry in literary manuscripts and periodicals across the country. Smith is now president of the Kalamalka Collective which publishes new poetry manuscripts every other year.

"Horsefaith" was based on backcountry horseback excursions in northwestern B.C.

below us
the glacier's grey tongue
bleeds into a bowl of green

silver braids split creeks in granite

we ride on a trail that
ribbons among wiry white pine
busy with wind

along the rock wall
that drops away from this ridge
two hawks
coast through circles
like flawless hangliders

one faltering hoof
would send us flailing and
kicking through hawk country

wingless flies
on a granite windshield

Joan Skogan

Joan Skogan has published a number of short stories and poems. While living in Prince Rupert she wrote *Skeena, A River Remembered* and *Princess and the Sea Bear*.

My mum's a reasonable woman. I know she is because she's always saying so. I'm only kidding. She is. Reasonable, I mean. Especially when you look at other mums who yell, "Because I say so. . . ." a lot of the time.

I don't know how she got Albert into the kitchen with her, though. He's not exactly a reasonable guy and it takes two to tango, she says. I know what she means even if I can't tango. Anyway, Albert was always making our yard his last stop on his way home. After he'd run out of kids to shove around on the street, he'd stop here.

This day Jason and I were painting the fort we were making out of the old chicken house. We were going to have a gang in there and the two of us were arguing about the password. Jason wanted "Argonauts" because of *Jason and the Argonauts*, which was a good movie and I have even read the book. My mum made me, but it was pretty good. But it was my fort. Why should he get to pick the password?

All that has nothing to do with what happened when Albert came up behind us and grabbed both brushes. I probably don't have to say what happened. It was one of those times when all you can do is wimp out and say, "I'm telling." I was on my own turf. And my mum was out of her workroom which she is glad to be after slaving over a hot typewriter all day, she says, and messing around, I found out later, with these pork and beans she is always trying and saying they will be as good as the ones in cans and they never are. But that has nothing to do with this story either.

Albert is about two feet taller than Jason and me put together. My mum looked out the window to see what was going on and was probably pissed off about the laundry right away, even though it was supposed to be water paint. She came out and said to Albert, "Can I talk to you for a minute?" She was polite and reasonable even for her but I don't know why Albert went with her. She stared at Jason and me until we went back into the fort and she took Albert inside with her. Jason kept asking me if she would smack him or at least tell his parents but I told him to give up hope on that.

When she tucked me in that night, which she still does most nights, and it doesn't bother me all that much, she told me what she did. "I gave him a few comps," she said in this especially patient voice she has when she wants to get away from me and read the paper but still be reasonable. She meant compliments, which she is always saying are more important to people than you realize until you remember how much you like them yourself. "And I asked him to consider being a hero. Now, good-night."

I figured there was more to it than that, but I wasn't going to get it out of her, and probably not out of Albert either. She never told me about the book for one thing, but Jason saw him shoving it inside his jacket when he left the yard.

I have to say that my mum is a writer and a nut about reading, especially for kids. She's always giving away books and telling kids they should read them. Sometimes I see the books lying on the street with their covers all wrinkly in the rain but I never tell her. She's happier not knowing. She would only go and have reasonable talks with the kids and it wouldn't do any good. Being reasonable is not the answer to everything.

Anyway, next day at lunchtime, Albert had the book stuck in his lunch bag and I got a sideways look at it. What do you know, it's *King Arthur and the Knights of the Round Table*, the one she had when she was a kid a hundred years ago. I'm only kidding. I was sort of mad though. She read it to me twice, and right when I saw it in Albert's lunch bag I felt like reading it again myself. I knew better than to say anything.

By now, I probably don't have to tell you that my mum would not have been reasonable about getting it back for me. No way. She would have talked about selfishness and greed and how they are human qualities to be fought wherever you find them, especially when you find them in yourself. Albert would never read the book anyway. Which shows you how little I knew. This is where the story really begins.

Albert's first try at being a Knight of the Round Table wasn't his fault. I know for sure all he meant to do was help Miss Ditson when she staggered into the room with an armload of our science reports. As far as I was concerned, they were no loss anyway. Mine would have been covered with her pointy red writing, saying things like "Research!" and "Spelling!" and "Handwriting!" None of which, except for the handwriting, which my mum said was a lot like Albert Einstein's, was my fault.

Our science report team was not a big success at team work. Connie and Alicia did their part of "Rainfall in Prince Rupert" on a word processor and wouldn't show any of it to Tom and me after we got kicked out of the library. The Good Librarian was not around at the time and the Bad Librarian called what we did "immature behaviour in connection with the library facilities." Which is just a fancy way of saying fooling around with the water fountain.

I said at the beginning it wasn't Albert's fault. All of us kids could see he never meant to trip Miss Ditson into the fish tank. He was only trying to get the pile of papers away from her to help carry them.

I figure even Miss Ditson didn't think Albert tripped her on purpose. But when he started mumbling about fair ladies and burdens, she called the principal. Seeing as the best thing Mr. Ward does is talk on the p.a. (he is on that thing about twenty times a day), he called the school psychologist. Albert had to talk to her every day.

Not completely a bad deal, in my opinion, since he got to miss choral singing. We were doing French rounds and stopping every minute or so to twist our mouths the way Mlle. Gruot showed us. Grotesque. Albert got sick of the psychologist though. He said she was always asking him about dreams and why he did perfectly ordinary stuff like tying Fat Morgan, who steals lunches, to the garbage can.

Anyway, the psychologist thing wasn't a dead loss because of course my mum found out about it and the whole thing led to a discussion between her and Albert and me. We were having Friday night supper, which is either macaroni and cheese or fish cakes. This is the only meal of the week when ketchup is allowed. Much later, Albert came to stay with us for a while. He brought his own ketchup bottle and kept it in his sleeping bag. My mum found out after four days. But that's another story.

Anyway, we talked about psychology. My mum is not bad to talk to. At least she's not always interrupting and thinking what she says is better than what you're saying. She says her life would be boring if she only had grown-ups in it.

Albert was telling about the school psychologist and we got onto dreams. Albert told a freaky one about blood and knives and big people going after little kids. It got sort of boring and some of it was from last week's movie, I bet. Albert gets to see a lot more movies than I do because he gets money from his dad every Friday night.

It was a big deal for Albert to give up his Friday night downtown for macaroni and cheese with us. He didn't seem too restless though. My mum went through the dream with him and it turned out pretty interesting. She thought a lot of it had to do with everyone being hunters in the forest a long ways back, and kids like me and Albert going through growing-up ceremonies. Here is maybe where the blood and knives come in.

Anyway, the hunting got us onto Robin Hood. We talked about him and his merry men and I could see Albert liked the idea of Robin Hood as much as I did. My mum read us a poem about Sherwood Forest, and she was really happy that Albert liked it. So happy that she let me go downtown with Albert after only ten minutes of talking about what streets we would use and all that. Be home by 9:00.

We weren't home by 9:00, but that was only because we ran into an old guy holding onto a bird with a broken wing right in front of the Empress. We tried helping him fix it with a rubber band but it was no good. The guy took the bird back into the beer parlour and I don't know what happened to it. But my mum got so interested she forgot to be mad. And she never did find out we'd been over at the new hotel and figured out how to get coke out of their machine without paying. That's all that happened that night.

The whole Robin Hood thing was different from King Arthur. For one thing, Albert told me about his plans. Simple. Rob the rich and give to the poor. We tried together at first. Not robbing, just looking for those chip packages with the free coupon on them. We must have picked up every bag on the south side, and I know that only two days ago some little kid in grade three found two of them in the same afternoon. We scored zero.

Next, Albert got me to help him look for pop bottles. Either the kids on Beach Place have expanded their territory or else the bag lady's been up our way, because we found exactly one. Which the lady at the Zippy Mart wouldn't take. She said it was dirty. Albert and I stared at each other, disgusted. I personally wondered what Robin Hood would have done. But we went behind the store and found a puddle to wash it off. I accidentally spilled some water, well, maybe more mud than water, on Albert's shoes. He got me in a hammer lock and thought about destroying me, I could see it on his face. But he let go. We finally got the bottle sort of clean and got a big ten cents with no smile from the store lady. We were so tired of trying to make money to give to the poor that we bought three jaw breakers with the dime. One each and half of number three. I let Albert chew it in half.

My mum didn't know anything about the rob the rich idea. We thought it was better that way. She kept on asking us if we wanted to hear more poems and sometimes it was tough getting away from her after school. She didn't seem all that surprised when the police phoned. Albert gave them our number. Not that his family has a phone anyway. They do have belts though, and once he showed me the marks from the time he lost the family allowance cheque. My mum stayed calm. She just said she'd be right down to the police station to pick him up.

I waited at home, trying not very hard to do my math questions. I wondered if they were going to keep Albert in a cell. Did they have little cells for kids? I was sort of looking forward to visiting him in there, maybe taking him some brownies with a chisel in them. Albert liked brownies better than cake, but I wasn't exactly sure what a chisel was.

The shop-lifting passed off with a lot of lectures to both of us and a few tears from everybody. My mum, Albert, and me, I mean. Albert's family, I think, never did find out about it. Mum explained to the police about Robin Hood and they took what she called a dim view of it. They said they didn't know what poor people would have done with two Bryan Adams tapes and a Ghostbusters sweat shirt. My mum was sad about the whole thing and really worried about Albert. We laid low for a while and she never mentioned reading anything else.

I saw *Treasure Island* lying beside her typewriter. But she went for a long walk last Saturday, down to the docks and through the train yard. She looked kind of thoughtful when she came back and she put *Treasure Island* away. I asked her myself if we could read *Tom Sawyer*, thinking it would cheer her up, you know. But she just looked at me really hard and said I could read it myself and keep it to myself.

She didn't really cheer up until Albert was finally allowed to stay overnight with us again and we got under the covers and left our feet on the pillows for her to tuck in. She laughed like anything. Albert stayed for the weekend and after a whole Saturday of doing normal stuff like going swimming and to the library, she asked him if he wanted to try reading again.

She told us she was going to hold back on *Kim* for a while, but she couldn't imagine that the the *Jungle Book* would do any damage. And it didn't at first. Albert and I took turns reading about Mowgli and the wolves who raised him and Bagheera and all the others. It was a great book. There wouldn't even be any more to this story if someone hadn't said there were wolves out at the dump. People are talking about going out to shoot them.

I know my mum will be reasonable about our plans. No matter how they turn out. She likes wolves a lot. Only last week, she was driving Albert and me to the skating rink and she put back her head at the stop sign and gave us a howl. She said if you practise long enough and get close enough to the wolves, they'll howl back at you. Albert and I are going try.

Grace Hols

Grace Hols writes fiction and poetry from her home in Houston, B.C. She has also worked as a feature reporter and newspaper editor and has won awards for her work in journalism as well as for her creative writing.

Most days except Sundays, Ma just fixed bread and cheese for lunch. On the counter, not bothering with the table. No tablecloth, no good dishes, that's for sure. Just a quick sandwich for me and Pa between running loads through the old wringer and sewing and canning and all that stuff she was so busy with back then in those early days, in the '50s.

One Wednesday, though, she started making lunch real early, 'way before the hands met at the top.

She stood on tiptoe to get the pretty blue cloth from the top shelf and floated it down over the kitchen table, bending over it to brush out all the lines and wrinkles. Then she put out the Sunday dishes we never even used most Sundays, and let me help blow off the dust. They made a soft clinking sound when she put them down on the blue cloth.

"We having a party?" I asked.

She shook her head and laughed a little like she had a secret.

"Who's coming?" I demanded, real nosy. Nobody ever came way over here, middle of the week.

She stopped polishing for a second and looked at me.

"A man is helping Dad today," she said, smiling, happy sounding. "A real Canadian."

"Not immigrant?" I was surprised. The only people we ever had over here were new arrivals like us.

Ma smiled even bigger. "A real Canadian," she repeated. *Een echte Canadese.* "Rich, too. He owns the bulldozer that is clearing our new field for oats." I had heard the dull roar of it outside all morning.

Then she stirred something on the stove and I smelled soup. She never made soup in the middle of the week.

She held out the egg basket to me. "Please go see if there are any fresh eggs today."

This was the first time she let me go to the chicken house by myself. I put on my rubber boots and an old coat over my homemade dress. I felt pretty big, but a little scared sticking my hand under the warm bellies of the chickens. There were six eggs, and I carried the basket carefully so they wouldn't break.

Ma cleaned the eggs and boiled them and put them in a bowl with a lacy cloth in the bottom. I had never seen her do that before. Eggs were for selling in town, she always said. She put the bowl on the table.

Then she opened the trap door on the floor and went down the little ladder to the dark, cool cellar. She came back with the butter in her hand. Butter was a special treat we had at Christmas and Easter and birthdays and sometimes on Sunday. The rest of the time we had margarine, that hard stuff that cracked when you tried to get it on your knife and that tore your bread when you wanted to spread it. She unwrapped the butter and put all of it in a fancy dish, the kind you could see through. Then she took a fork and made designs on the top, swirling and wavy. She stood back from the counter to look at it, her hands on her hips and her head first this way, then that. She made more designs. The butter looked too pretty to eat when she finally set it on the table.

She put her new pink blouse on, fixed her hair, and put on lipstick. Three times she went to the window to see if they were coming.

I touched the eggs to see if they were still hot. I reached out to touch the butter, too, but Ma got mad.

"Get away from that table," she hissed. *Blijf van die tafel.* She shooed me into the corner with my crayons and papers.

I couldn't figure it.

Finally the roar of the big machine stopped. A few minutes later there was stomping on the porch. The door opened. Pa stood there, brushing off sawdust and old leaves and dirt. Beside him stood a man I had never seen before. He was tall and dark looking and filled the doorway like a thunder-cloud, with hair over most of his face and lots sticking out under his hat. His shirt was as dirty as Pa's but he just left it be. He came in with his boots on. Hat, too.

"Hello!" Ma said in English. She was smiling lots and I didn't like the way she sounded, kind of shy and sucky at the same time. She always sounded like that when she spoke to someone who wasn't immigrant like us. When she got groceries she sounded sucky, too, and called the check-out girls "Ma'am." Yes, Ma'am. Thank you, Ma'am. They were Canadians. We weren't.

The man grunted something back without looking at Ma.

We prayed before we ate the way we always did.

"Our Father. . . ." began Pa. I kept my head down, but opened my eyes a little. Ma had her eyes squeezed crinkly shut and her fingers were folded so tight the knuckles were white. The man, the Canadian, had his elbows on the table and his hands not even folded. He looked this way and that around the kitchen, turning his head like an old owl. I ducked my head down even more and shut my eyes so he wouldn't catch me peeking.

"Soup, sir?" asked Ma, standing, the red ladle in her hand. She sounded silly, like she'd been practising.

The man lifted his shoulders some. "Sure," he said.

She filled his bowl. He ate right away, not waiting for us, and making lots of slurping noises, the kind I usually got slapped for. But Ma didn't even notice.

He ate lots. He loved Ma's homemade bread. She cut more for him and he put plenty of butter on each piece. Ma made me some bread and butter, too, but she put it on real thin like she always did so it would last longer.

The man talked lots when he was eating.

"She started workin' a lot better with that new kinda oil," he said to my Pa. I watched his mouth and I saw the food there and I wondered why none of it fell out when he spoke. He had holes where some teeth should have been. "You shoulda seen her smoke last week." He kept talking even though Ma was refilling his coffee cup. "She been pretty good so far. No big breakdowns or nothin'. But I gotta get them treads rebuilt pretty quick." Coffee spilled on the blue cloth when he lifted the cup to his mouth.

Pa listened carefully, his eyes partly squinty like he was having a hard time understanding. He didn't say much. Just grinned and nodded lots. Pa could be kind of sucky, too.

The Canadian banged his fist on the table. "Just four more payments and she's all mine," he said, proud and sticking his chest out.

We all finished eating 'way before the man put down his knife.

"Will you have more, sir?" Ma asked, shy and extra nice. I wished she would stop talking like that. She didn't even talk that way to our minister. But he was immigrant, too, like us.

The bulldozer man shook his head and leaned back on his chair until it sat on two legs.

"Nope," he said. "Time to get back to work, I figger."

He burped, not even covering his mouth. I looked at Ma real quick, but she was busy with the soup ladle.

Pa stood up. Ma, too. She waited until the men walked around the table and out of the door. Pa turned and smiled at Ma and gave me a little wave. The man did not say a thing to Ma or me. He was busy talking to Pa about once when he almost rolled his machine off the side of a hill.

There was dirt under the chair where he sat.

Ma started to clear the table. She wrapped up what was left of the butter and brought it back to the cellar. She piled up the dishes carefully and brushed the crumbs off the blue cloth. She hummed a little tune and smiled to herself.

I ran over to the window and watched Pa and the Canadian walking back to the bulldozer.

I wanted to bang on the window.

Hey mister, I wanted to yell. I went to the chicken house for eggs. We used our Sunday dishes, I wanted to say, and Ma put designs in the butter.

Dina von Hahn

Dina von Hahn lives in Terrace, B.C. where she teaches English part-time, enjoys her house and garden, and vows to spend more time writing. Between 1985 and 1990 she worked as a journalist in northwestern B.C. and the Yukon.

There's an open-line show on
the cab radio as we drive
into town in the dark.
They're talking about Joe Hazelwood
and what his sentence was
and what it should have been.

The next day a guy on the docks says
the spill was great for him
personally.
It meant a job and a chance to see Alaska.

In the café they're lined up
to eat eggs and bacon
at the counter.
The woman serving looks at me
with suspicion,
wondering if I'll come back.

A young guy says it hurt the fishing
he'd like to see Hazelwood out
scrubbing rocks.

But the woman says
everyone is to blame.

Deanna Kawatski

Deanna Kawatski's words first broke into print in a poetry collection published by Fiddlehead in 1980. Her feature articles have appeared in magazines such as *Harrowsmith, Canadian Gardening, Country Journal,* and *Mother Earth News.* Residents of northern B.C. for many years, she and her children now live at Shuswap Lake.

"Natty Creek Garden Journal" is the final segment of a garden journal series written for *Country Journal,* and appears in part in Ms Kawatski's newest book, *Wilderness Mother* (Whitecap Books).

November 14: Nightly a visitor has been crossing the garden, leaving deep tracks in the snow. Last evening, my daughter Nat stepped onto the front porch and switched on the spotlight, and a wolf was trotting lightly across the buried clover field. Halted by the blast of brightness, he stared up at the house with eyes that glowed supernaturally in the light.

This morning, I was in the outhouse that overlooks Natty Creek. I was mulling over a sobering fact that I had learned while reading James Lovelock's *Gaia* — that the troposphere upon which all species are totally dependent for survival, is only seven miles wide! Shivering from the coldness that was seeping into my bones, I felt acutely aware of the fragility of the narrow rind of life encompassing the planet. Slowly I became conscious of someone watching me through the glassless window. My eyes were drawn to a spot just beyond the garden. There, a light-coloured wolf lay regarding me with cool curiosity. Then he stood up on long sinewy legs and shook a great cloud of snow from his hide. I held my breath as he stared back at me a while longer, moved further off, shook again, and vanished into the trees.

November 26: An early rising. It snowed last night, and the spruce rounds that my husband Jay hauled and piled in the yard are wrapped in a four-inch muffler of white. The stars are winking and the air is warmer. He cut the standing dead tree past the west end of the garden. Kneeling lithely on the seatless skidoo with its half-a-tin-bathtub hood, in 'coonskin' cap, he looked like a Davy Crockett on wheels as he roared across the garden, avoiding the perennial beds. Ben, our youngest, sat flat on the home-made sled that whipped obediently around the corners and across the bridge, his feet encased in pink boots passed down from Nat. Whenever they charged back again, with the narrow sled piled high, Ben was draped over the top of the load, hanging on tight, loving every minute of it.

November 28: Jay has acquired a wood lathe this winter, and it's established itself in the front room. It is now necessary to squeeze by it and flying chips and sawdust — past a husband not only prematurely aged but mummified by dust, the eyes through the plastic safety goggles glittering like a deep sea diver's upon discovering a treasure — to get out the front door. Sanding sends up a blizzard of dust that coats the shelves, the stove, the rug, the dog. All matter grows mossy with it. The house plants are suffocating. Even upstairs, I have to blow on my sweaters in order to identify them. Now and then the kids and I cough, and Jay is thinking of ordering dust masks from the wood supply catalogue. The noise makes it seem like the whole house is a giant tooth that's being drilled. He'll also order ear plugs. Granted, the birch, alder, and willow containers that he's turning out are marvellous.

November 30: The sky is vibrating with the motion of large flocks of winter birds. The snow is scattered with birch seeds and the minute seed eaters — including crossbill, siskins, redpolls, and juncos — pulsate as single bodies from birch clump to alder stand. Their song is welcome in the shrinking days of winter when the deciduous trees stand rigid as wrought iron against the pale sky.

Nat and I went for a walk. The fresh snow was richly embroidered with squirrel and mouse trails which Nat guarded with fierce backward glances, insisting that I not step on any of the minute passageways. They vanished into tiny round tunnels in the snowbanks, and we could only imagine all of the animal activity going on hidden from view. What if a mouse and weasel bumped noses on their meanderings through the white maze? I suspect that the weasel, lean and wily, and ever the predator, would win out over a white-footed deer mouse, the likes of whom I've discovered in the cupboard, hiding head with paws and trembling. And I can just hear the chatter of a squirrel chancing upon a ruffed grouse burrowed into the snow, and see the explosion of bird flapping for the nearest tree, and scatter of squirrel back down the tunnel.

December 4: Millions of snowflakes flickered down all day yesterday. The weather box is wearing a ridiculously large cap of white. When I check the temperatures with a faltering flashlight, it's 0° Fahrenheit, and a near full moon glows in the southwest. Strange creatures have swelled up where once there was a wood stack, teeter totter, and wheelbarrow.

Bears, woodchucks, and bats aren't the only local creatures that curl up in their caves for the season. We also stay inside more and burrow into our winter projects. I'm writing regularly and knitting Nat a sweater. Nat studies and sketches compulsively. Jay built Ben a desk and Ben keeps his 'treasures' locked inside, and wears the key on a piece of cord around his neck.

At present, Jay and Ben are in Stewart and Nat and I are in charge of the animals. The one product that we're still getting from the garden is hay. Nat and I stop to flop in the snow, making angels, on our way to the last of the three hay mounds that stand draped in white like a Halloween ghost.

December 6: Overnight our world has turned drab, slanted by rain that deflates the snow and saddens the trees. The rabbits weather well in winter. They simply stay still, conserving energy for growing more fur. Two does, Button and Sassafras, peek at us from behind their nest of hay, anxious to see what's next on the menu. They're on a three-day hay-potato-turnip cycle.

I climb into the centre of the hay hive that is built around four strips of wood that join together at the top, supported by crosspieces. Inside, it is redolent with the aroma of hay blended with wild mint and clover. There's crouching space only and beneath the snow, around the outside, lies an unsavoury rind of mouldy hay. This has proven lethal to rabbits and we're careful to give them only the healthy stuff from inside. Tugging at the tightly packed straw we cram the buckets full five times, one for each cage containing two bunnies.

Later: We were expecting Jay and Ben home tonight and they haven't come. Jay is never late, and I can't help but worry. When Nat and I went out in the icy downpour to check the weather, there was already an inch of rain in the gauge. I suddenly remembered the dam, and we rushed down the slippery hill in the blackness. The tiny flashlight cast a weak eye on a grim situation. The water was lifting its burden of ice up to the top of the bank. To add intrigue to the scenario, a trail of very fresh wolf tracks crossed a corner of the pond, distinct rosettes in the melting ice. The centre spillway, from which we had to remove a board, was buried under two feet of sodden snow. We laid on our bellies and stared upside-down at the arrangement, shouting over the roar of angry water. Fumbling up the hill like the blind, we retrieved shovel, crowbar, and work gloves. Agitated, I forgot the design of the spillway, and level-headed Nat had to explain it to me.

Back at the dam, Nat held the flashlight while I shovelled, throwing the leaden chunks over the spillway. Finally we located the two eight-foot boards that had to be removed, and with much additional shovelling and wrestling, we pried them out of place. Footing above the swirling water was precarious and at one point I came close to falling in. As it was, we were soaked from the rain. The other board that had to be removed was submerged in water and, flat on my belly — after several attempts with the crowbar — I felt a great surge, and Nat grabbed the board to keep it from being washed away. The release of water was matched only by our surge of relief. The dam was safe!

December 9: Still no Jay and Ben, and my mind is going wild from worry. "How long have they been gone?" I ask Nat and she calculates: "Let's see — hay, potatoes, turnips, hay, potatoes, turnips. Six days!" They're three days late, and I'm ready to throw the radio telephone through the window. It's been out of order for three months. We keep our ears glued to regular radio, anxious for any news of the Northwest, and it's as though this corner of the province doesn't even exist!

December 10: They came across the yard last night, looking like ghosts in the flashlight. It turned out that the road was closed due to avalanche conditions, and Jay and Ben were stuck in Stewart for an extra four days. Right now, I don't want them to ever go away again!

December 13: Despite the mild cold Ben picked up in town, I took him skiing across the garden today. It takes some patience to poke along behind him while he hits the snow yet another time and gets his skis twisted up in ways that defy natural law. However, a friendly word is all that it takes to restore his balance and he wears the perpetual white patch on the seat of his snowpants with nonchalance.

Later he came into the root cellar with me and when his eyes fell on the carrot bin, where the bright roots are sending forth anaemic tops, he marvelled, "The carrots are growing!"

Supper tonight was simple but succulent. This morning I grabbed a frozen rabbit from the smokehouse. Later I peeled potatoes, carrots, onions, and garlic; and arranged them in and around the rabbit, roasting the works for about three hours. Leftovers will be made into soup.

December 14: While skiing along the river, Nat and I were delighted to see no less than eight reputedly solitary dippers. I've read that this plump stub-tailed relative of the wren is the only aquatic songbird in North America. It is fun to watch them do their rhythmic squats on shelves of ice extending precariously out over swift green water. Nat and I shivered as one dove unflinchingly into the main current. In fact, I once saw one make twenty consecutive dives, three to six seconds apart. Winging through the water, they then walk along the bottom in search of small fish, insects, and aquatic invertebrates. Swooping low over the current, dippers never stray far from the water that they worship in song all winter long. It is startling to hear such a lilting melody in the hushed and introverted whiteness of winter.

December 21: My soul sings in celebration of Winter Solstice and the passing of the shortest day of the year as I bake bread and clean for Christmas. The cookie tins are filled to the brim with gingerbread men, shortcake, fruit cake, pecan dreams, and sugar cookies. These, together with the metal chest of *lebkuchen* from Berlin, and the cookies from Dorothy Zide in Kentucky, are more than enough for family and friends.

The temperature has been down to -18° Fahrenheit and the breath hangs like moss on the biting air. The sun is at its most elusive phase, as though without the energy required to rise above the mountain peaks. Instead it skims the ridges, transforming trailing cloud to luminous manes. After an hour of direct light when the valley is once again bathed in optimism, the sun spins behind South Mountain, emerging from the far side in the late afternoon. After twenty minutes, it sinks without resistance behind the spires of tall spruce. The coldest weather will come within the next month.

Jay is making a skating rink on the pond while Nat and Ben eagerly count the days until Christmas. Nestled in our remote valley, we happily escape most of the crass commercialism of the season. However it's difficult to rejoice fully when a major military confrontation may at any moment break out in the Persian Gulf. Of equal concern is the ever-intensifying war that industrial civilization has been waging against nature for the past two centuries. It is appalling that we continue minute by minute, day by day, to kill our own mother, the Earth, when we need her and what's left of her diverse life expressions, as much as a foetus needs a womb. Without profound change and compassion, the wounds will never heal.

December 26: The last of this year's tomatoes sit in a small bowl on the counter. Christmas has come and gone. Boxing Day is mild and encased in cloud, an opaque presence above the garden. A festive feeling lingers on, fuelled by music from the electronic keyboard that my mother sent.

We shared Christmas with the Handel family and Scott, a single fellow from the highways camp. In the morning, the kids skated while I stuffed the roosters that were hatched in our incubator in August. I used the last of the celery from the root cellar, and home-grown sage and thyme.

The afternoon was filled with games, laughter, and some sloppy carol singing. Later in remembrance of Christmases past, I spread the red cloth that mom used when I was a child. Then Nat, Clara, Julie, and I snuck upstairs and put on dresses. The main course was roast chicken, mashed potatoes, giblet gravy, low-bush cranberry sauce, Brussels sprouts, and dill pickles, all grown locally. Dessert was carrot pudding. Before digging in, we joined hands briefly, forming a ring of thanks for the gifts of life and health on this lone green planet of the universe.

December 31: The garden is transformed to a fairy-land by a full moon and fresh snow. My boots squeak out a curious tune as I trudge across the pristine ivory quilt, revelling in nature's handiwork. Rather than conceal, the snow accentuates the contours of the rows, and every rise and fold is scattered with thousands of lunar jewels. When I stop on the small bridge, the only sound is the fluid muttering of Natty Creek that hurries on while minnows of moonlight dart across her surface. Above, the silver orb seems snagged in the branches of a spiny alder, its black fingers laden with the crystal fruit of winter. The raspberry canes are bowing to the power of the season that has invaded. Brown lily stalks stand, their spent glory clutching snow, and I think of words by Carl Jung:

> *Life has always seemed to me like a plant that lives on its rhizome. The part that appears above ground lasts only a single summer. Then it withers away — an ephemeral apparition. When we think of the unending growth and decay of life and civilization, we cannot escape the impression of absolute nullity. Yet, I have never lost a sense of something that lives and endures underneath the eternal flux. What we see is the blossom, which passes. The rhizome remains.*

Snowy spruce bows become angel wings, some pointing earthward, others skyward while the towering trees cast shadows the full length of the garden. On this magical evening, I am left wishing whimsically that our species could feed exclusively on the natural beauty that the planet still abounds with, for it opens the door to truth and love, and it is truly the food of our souls. Without it our souls will wither.

As I climb the hill to the sleeping house, the soaring mountains are marbled by light while a pink ring appears around the moon and a tide of diaphanous star-flecked cloud sweeps across the southern sky. In the garden that breathes deep beneath its bed of snow blossoms, the rhizome remains.

Le Patinage Noir (On Frozen Pond)

Lynda Orman

Lynda Orman grew up at Sauble Beach on Lake Huron. A marine biologist, she lives and works in Prince Rupert, BC. She has been involved with the Prince Rupert Writers' Group since its inception in 1981.

I'm wearing thin,
thin as ice
You are the blade that cuts across my surface
Le patinage noir
severing my throat
my wrists
I may bleed to death
unless a premature thaw
melts this frozen pond

Iain Lawrence

Iain Lawrence writes a weekly newspaper column in Prince Rupert, B.C. He spends the summers travelling the coast in a small sailboat, and much of his writing centres on the sea. A contributor to *Pacific Yachting* magazine, he has written a sailing guide to the North Coast that is due for publication in 1995.

Grandpa was a seafaring man. He could tell stories about bloodthirsty pirates and storms at sea and cruel captains by the dozen.

He'd been around the world at least thirty times, and he once took a clipper ship single-handed around Cape Horn during the worst storm in two centuries.

Auntie Mae said the closest Grandpa ever came to rounding Cape Horn was the time he got blown off the edge of the old Ocean Dock in a December gale. But she didn't know Grandpa like I did. Grandpa was a sailor. He had a pair of seaboots in his bedroom closet, big black boots with the tops rolled down and loops of tarry string to hold them in place.

"I wasn't any older than you when I signed aboard the old *Hispaniola* and put on them boots for the first time," he told me. I could put both feet into one boot and hold the top up around my waist. "Well, maybe I was a bit older than you," he said. "But I was a big 'un for my age. Always was."

The story of the *Hispaniola* was one of Grandpa's favourites. It took him every night of a cold November to tell me how, as a boy, he'd helped sail the ship in search of buried treasure and battled off a whole gang of pirates, including one with a wooden leg. He told me the story in little pieces, always breaking off just when it was getting exciting. It wasn't until several years later that I learned Grandpa had been memorizing sections of *Treasure Island* during the day.

Some of his other stories were like that, too. It turned out that he had never hunted the Great White Whale. Nor had he navigated the Ulanga River in a tiny steamboat called the *African Queen*. But a young boy can disregard facts better than a religious fanatic, and even Grandpa believed his stories at the time of their telling.

I spent hours sitting in my little rocking chair while Grandpa rambled on about mutinies and the women of the south seas and the numerous times he had come across the Flying Dutchman in her ghostly voyaging. Sometimes he'd step into his seaboots, pull on his long navy duffel-coat and watchcap and stomp up and down his bedroom floor, bellowing orders to invisible crewmen.

"Bring in those topsails, there," he'd shout. "And get a reef in that main to'gallant before she blows herself to pieces. Look lively, you slovenly bunch of barnacles or I'll have you swinging by the yardarm at dawn, by gum!"

He'd send the men aloft in the worst of weather, with the ship heeled over so far he had to stagger along the deck and grab onto the bedposts for support. It wasn't until he saw the sails set just right, a process that could take half an hour at times, that he would allow me to risk a turn at the wheel.

"Watch your heading, boy," he'd say. "She's going to luff up if you're not careful."

Then he'd go below for a sleep, leaving me to navigate by the feel of the wind on my face and the light of the ceiling lamp. And I'd look forward, not over a bedroom floor but over a wooden deck gleaming with salt spray, and see the rows and tiers of canvas sails billowing above me. It was part of Grandpa's magic, an art he'd learned in the West Indies where the natives had taught him how to make men see what he wanted them to see.

"I could tell you some of the things I've seen down in that part of the world," he said. "But there wouldn't be no point because you wouldn't believe them anyway. Why I've seen those fellows chop the heads off chickens and keep the bodies alive for months, dropping bits of food down their gullets."

"Why would they want to do that?" I asked. And Grandpa laughed and stroked his moustache with one of his huge, brown hands.

"Well that way the chickens didn't have any brains, you see. And they wouldn't think of trying to escape or nothin'."

"Could they put ships in bottles?" I asked.

"Oh, yes," said Grandpa. "But not the way you're used to seeing. They could take real ships and shrink them down complete with crew and everything."

"Could you do that, Grandpa?"

"Well, it's been years since I tried that, boy," he said. "But I've likely got a couple of empty bottles lying around here and I just might give it a try."

Grandpa set to work the next day, carving tiny hulls and fitting them with miniature masts and spars. His knotted hands, like two burlap bags of bones, fitted elaborate riggings of thread and stretched tiny cotton sails over the yards.

He never showed me how to put the ships inside the bottle. I woke up one morning three weeks later to find it already done, the bottle sitting on my bedside table.

Inside, two frigates were beating to windward over a grey, foam-streaked sea. Both ships were close-hauled and colourful pennants fluttered from the mastheads.

"That one there's my old ship, the *Indefatigable*," he said, pointing to the ship furthest back in the bottle. She's trying to run down that Frenchie and get a clear shot at her. That chase lasted for days."

Grandpa came down with an awful sickness that week and Auntie Mae put him straight to bed with a bowl of soup and a mustard plaster. Grandpa said he'd been confined to quarters, and I carried the ship in a bottle into his bedroom where I could sit beside his bed.

He lay quietly, with his eyes half open, and I sat holding the bottle in my lap. The neck was sealed with tarred rope braided into fancy knots. And it seemed that the smell of the sea was leaking out between the strands.

Every hour or so, Grandpa would stir in his bed and ask me how the old *Indefatigable* was making out in her chase.

"The weather's worsening," he said quietly, without shifting his head. "That'll help her a bit. Always could sail better to windward than those Frenchies."

I looked inside the bottle and I thought that the waves were a little higher than they had been. That the sails were a little fuller. And the ships had become almost immeasurably closer together.

"She's gaining," I said. Grandpa smiled and his lips looked cold and grey.

"You watch 'em," he said. "You watch 'em, boy."

I balanced the bottle on the seat of the chair and knelt down on the carpet, my face pressed so close to the glass that my breath covered the bottle with fog. And each time I wiped the mist away the little world inside the bottle had changed.

Both ships were heeled a little more, as though the wind was strengthening. Gunports were opened and cannons were run out. The bowsprit of the French ship dug deeply into the seas.

"You watch 'em, boy," Grandpa said in a voice I could hardly hear.

The ships started to shorten sail. The tiny cotton rectangles were furled one by one along the yards, streaks of foam blew across the surface of the sea, and the *Indefatigable* drew increasingly closer to the Frenchman.

Auntie Mae carried me to my own bed late the second day. I fell asleep as the *Indefatigable* fired its first shots to test the range.

Sometime that night, Grandpa died. And in the morning only one ship was left in the bottle, its little wooden hull scarred by cannon shots, its mizzen mast snapped in two.

And behind the wheel of the old *Indefatigable* was a tiny figure with seaboots and a navy duffel-coat.

Grandpa will always be a seafaring man.

George Stanley

George Stanley was born and raised in San Francisco. A former Northwest Community College instructor in Terrace, George now lives in Vancouver. His poetry has been published in a number of collections including *Gentle Northern Summer* and *Four Realities: Poets of Northern BC* (Caitlin Press).

That the world have no meaning,
no purpose, a top set in motion,

but that Nanabush be there, off & on,
a bird flying in yr face, to remind you

that is the meaning.

(Like the nun used to come
soundlessly up the aisle
& get you
                    behind the ear
w/her knuckle)

Is it really my job
to go through these files
(R. being on vacation),
if it don't lead me, permanently,
to a staircase to heaven?

Each of them looking back at you says
I am here for a lifetime, so are you,
& the new ones
                    come on
                              while you
have time to think about it.

STANLEY

If you forget any of this,
I will time & time again remind you.
I will be shooting star, opening tulip

& also snowfall.

*see *The Rez Sisters*, by Tomson Highway

Sheila Peters

Sheila Peters has lived with her family just outside Smithers, B.C. since 1977 except for a two-year stint in Prince George where she wrote for a local magazine. She writes poetry and fiction, and teaches writing at Northwest Community College. She is presently working on her first novel.

I sat at my kitchen table laboriously folding an origami rowboat. I had bought a book demonstrating the nautical equivalent of the art of folding paper airplanes. Ostensibly for my children, the book was really for me. I love following the instructions, figuring out the folds and angles, producing a perfectly engineered ship from a leftover scrap of paper.

I needed an excuse, however. A Mother's Day present lay waiting to be wrapped, and I decided to decorate it with paper boats. So, naturally, I started thinking about water, my mother, and — inevitably — swimming.

I was a child and the sea was home to my body. Its salt supported me as I thrashed my way to buoyancy; it cleansed my scrapes and cuts; it washed illness away. My mom never took us to the beach and said, "Now, don't get wet." Yes, I have seen this, have heard parents tell their children they can't go swimming because they have a cold. Or it wasn't warm enough.

Why were they there, I wondered, if not to swim? To torment their children? I was an adult before I understood that people go to the beach for reasons other than swimming.

My family firmly believed that swimming in the ocean, even in cool water, was a tonic; refreshing and curative. It would certainly never cause any harm.

Perhaps I should clarify here that it was my mom's family, weaned on North Sea beaches, who made the summer evening trips down the terraced streets of Powell River to the beach. Since we lived farthest away, my mom would begin the walk with just the three of us kids in tow. On the way down towards the water we would pick up Granny, and sometimes Grandpa, and then join our aunt and her three children at the beach just below her house. But the sons-in-law, men who worked outside on log booms summer and winter, day shift and night shift, were intent on keeping their bodies out of the salt chuck; it would take more than a warm, idle summer evening to re-route those neural paths.

Unnecessary modesty was scorned on these outings. We changed behind boulders or the massive roots of beached cedars, struggling to pull clothes over damp salty skin before a shielding towel fell or was blown away. My grandfather would change beneath a towel even at the most public beach on a Saturday afternoon. One summer, while his wife was back in Scotland, my mom had to force him to buy a new bathing suit; his old one was so full of holes it was no longer decent. In his late seventies at that time, thin, wrinkled, and almost blind, he appeared the next day in brilliant blue satin trunks, their cut clearly intended for young hunks. It was, I think, his last bathing suit.

As I grew and was exposed to a wider array of summer social activities, I was astonished to discover that many people didn't like to swim at all, and of those who did, most preferred lakes. Or, as wealth grew, swimming pools.

As for myself, I have never trusted fresh water. Not even swimming pools. The sight of small children toddling along the slippery tiles, a stumble away from eight or ten unforgiving feet of bleached water, makes me cringe. What will happen if I leave before their sundazed parents wake up? Or if the lifeguard is distracted by a teenage commotion?

But watching children play beside the ocean is as comforting as seeing them curled up, dozing in the sun against salty women's skin.

The beach at the bottom of Third Avenue where we used to swim was protected and benign. I could not fall in off the edge; at high tide there were no sudden drops, just enough slope so the water got comfortably deep before I was too far away from my mom for reassurance. The ocean could not carry me off because each wave pushed me back to shore. Its secrets were revealed at every tide's ebb, its furtive crabs and limp slippery weeds, its smooth stones and gravel washed twice daily, as orderly as my own ablutions.

There were no rip tides, no undercurrents, just waves, logs to ride and dive from, and buoyant salt cradling young bodies. It seemed to me the only people the ocean claimed were those foolish enough to go too far from shore, and then what could you expect? Storms, too much drink, holes in boats, these killed people. Not swimming.

Because we live so far from the ocean now, and my need for immersion is so strong, my children learned to swim in lakes. But growing comfortable with lakes has taken me years. There were oceans for swimming and puddles for puddling. On the clearest calmest day the ocean never reflected anything but fractured light. Lakes, being fresh water, were closer, in my family's pantheon, to puddles. Not entirely clean and reflecting a different kind of light. A child peering in, wonders how deep is this puddle, are my rubber boots tall enough or will the water rise to slip over the rims? Then seeing the whole sky waiting in that calm reflection, the depth unimaginable, the child teeters terrified at the edge while feeling that pull down, down into the sky.

Haslam Lake, one of the lakes of my childhood, was like that. Still, limpid water reflected trees that crept right up and hung over its edges.

As for unclean, well, it's not really fair to call Haslam Lake dirty — it supplied much of the town with wonderful drinking water. But when I was younger and still afraid of lakes, its squishy bottom, sludged stones, and logs dead beneath the accumulation of eons sent a ripple of distaste up my spine. Like cold, greasy cutlery at the bottom of a sink full of forgotten dishwater.

To avoid the ooze, we'd swim at a gravelly patch of shoreline resembling the seashore at high tide. And here the lake revealed its true nature; it was a cheap trick, a watery imitation lacking substance and buoyancy. Floating took effort; concentration wavered into floundering panic. All confidence in my fledgling dog paddle dissolved in flailing, sputtering indignity. Because of this, I disliked lakes. As well as muddy, tangled with weeds, hiding leeches of legendary awfulness, they were mean-spirited and dangerous.

Sometimes my mom took us to Haslam Lake fishing — not often, but once or twice. We'd rent a rowboat from a man with goats — the only person who lived on the lake. He must have lived there for years, before people worried about water supplies and had referendums on fluoridation.

We rented the rowboat for forty cents an hour, $1 for two and a half hour's fishing. Plenty of time.

I don't remember anyone catching fish. Mom would tell one of us to be ready to take her line if the fisheries officers came by — but I never saw a fisheries officer deal with anything as insignificant as fresh water until I moved here to the Bulkley Valley, where salmon and those elusive steelhead battle their way beyond the tides, past the jealousy and treachery of fishermen and sloughing riverbanks.

The road to Haslam Lake was gravel and darkened by overhanging alder and salmonberry bushes. Above this impenetrable barrier the cedar and hemlock pressed in. Other roads led off to marshy Duck Lake and beyond to the preserves of more serious outdoorsmen. But the road to Haslam Lake curved left past the filtration dam, past the goat farm.

It wasn't a real farm, just a shack on a strip of land between the lake and the road, a strip of stumps and logs strewn across bright mossy grass cropped close by the goats. The goats would assume crazy perches on the stumps and run nimbly through the debris as we drove down to the dock of silvered boards.

When we were a little older, we'd ride our bikes up to Haslam Lake to fish or swim on our own. Later still, equipped with driver's licences, we'd drive up there in our robin's egg blue 1960 Vauxhall station wagon with forty ("count them!" we'd laugh) horsepower. It was our first car. My mom and all of us kids learned to drive in it.

Braver now, we'd follow a narrow path to swim back beneath a rocky bluff. This was the place where Neil MacKenzie dove and broke his neck like in a gruesome summer safety film strip. Or was it his back? But he lived and walked and married and has children — I never did understand about broken necks and backs — I always thought it was instant death or paralysis, and yet there are people alive and seemingly well. . . .

We measured our nerve, our maturity, against swimming holes. Powell Lake was a step up. It was a home fit for all the monsters of a child's imagining. Swollen by a dam and spotted with deadheads, it was deep, prehistorically deep. Some claimed that there was salt water trapped at the bottom beneath layers and layers of unmoving lake water. And I remember hearing there were spots where they couldn't find the bottom at all. I would imagine skillful, serious men out there in a rowboat, paying out mile after tedious mile of thin line, taut and heavy as it was pulled down into the sky reflected in the lakecalm surface.

Let's face it. Lakes are creepy.

But they're amateur freshwater villains compared to silent, sliding rivers. My children play beside and fish in the Bulkley River, one that has claimed many lives on its sweep to Prince Rupert. There are countless stories of fishermen slipping off its treacherous rocks; a mother's nightmares lurk beneath the mercury sheen of its water.

There is a story of a woman parking on the river bank across the road from a pay phone. Leaving her sleeping two-year-old in the back seat to make a short call, she returned minutes later to find his footprints emerging from the other side of the car, leading to the edge of the ice.

They never found him.

I remember reading another story of a man, helpless, watching his young son slip off a bridge into a river just east of here. He, too, was lost.

I know these sound like stories invented by nervous mothers to frighten children into obedience. But they were reported in the local paper; they are not parents' imagined terrors. No imaginings can outdo what really happens.

So I clutch my children's hands as we stand and peer off bridges and cliffs into the river to see spawning salmon. And, as they grow older, I try to swallow my fear and recreate the same waterside peace my mom gave to me. One spring day I had to walk away as their father and a friend stood with them on a bridge, throwing stones into the creek far below — walk away with my hands shoved deep into pockets to keep from grabbing them, pulling them from the edge.

You see, lakes are bad enough, but I've had no practice with real rivers, no practice at all. Powell River, the community that is, has no seriously moving water. There were only two bridges I can recall, both over rivers dammed to produce hydroelectricity for the pulp and paper mill. One spanned the memory of Powell River itself, swallowed between the dam above the mill and the brooding lake. The other crossed the shrivelled remnants of Eagle River on the south end of the forty miles of highway between Lund and the ferry out of town, the boundaries of our restlessness. Eagle River drained a chain of lakes filled with ghostly trees, erect and dead in the water.

Below the dam, what remained of the river trickled through swimming holes joined by waterfalls, surrounded by cliffs. This is where we came when hormones sent us jangling down the highway on summer afternoons. By then we were crammed into a friend's Volkswagen, listening to Paul McCartney's "Lalalalalalovely Linda."

It was upstream in this same river, in a frigid pool in the tumble of huge debris just below the dam, that we proved our sophistication by swimming naked. Perhaps swimming is overstating it. The leap from rocks to water lasted longer than the panicked scramble to reach shore and huddle shivering under towels.

But behind these tame river adventures was the knowledge the warning horn could go off at any second signalling a release of water from the dam, turning the emasculated trickle into its true river self, a spectacle none of us had witnessed.

The fear was real. One time we climbed back through the bush to the dam itself and walked across. No handrailings shielded us from the bulk of water it restrained, from the terror of the long concrete sweep to the sharp jumble of boulder far below. So we played with one ear alert for freshwater treachery.

I never did hear that horn, and I realize now there was little likelihood of ever hearing it in the dryness of summer. But who thought of such things then? The town faced the ocean and its water levels were as predictable as the moon. We had no knowledge of the ways of rivers.

So, the familiar ocean was where we went for safety, to hide from adults, light fires, talk, drink, and swim in the warm black summer phosphorescence. The beach was a path you could walk without fear of ever getting lost.

Every family has its rituals for reassurance. In ours, getting dunked is a matter of ceremony and virtue. There are clear rules, procedures. If one toe goes in the water, the rest of the body must follow. Or rather, if you get your bathing suit on and go down to the beach, you have to get wet, even if you don't stay in.

I do my best to maintain this tradition, and make a point of swimming wherever I can. I have swum in the Atlantic and the Pacific, the Mediterranean and the Caribbean, the Aegean and the Andaman, the Gulf of Mexico and the English Channel, the Bay of Biscay and the Adriatic, the Tyrrhenian and the Ionian, the Straits of Juan de Fuca and Malaspina, the Gulf of California and the Yucatan Canal, Hecate Strait and Desolation Sound. Overcoming my freshwater prejudices, I have swum in Lakes Ontario, Huron, and Superior, though I'm afraid of the polluted soup of Lake Erie. (If its water had been salt, however, I may well have held my nose and swam.) I have shrieked and shivered in countless glacial streams and lakes. I have even swum in back eddies of the Bulkley River, though I cannot bear to watch my family fish at its edge.

I have a friend who shares this desire to swim in every body of water that presents itself. We used to have our most intense conversations treading water out beyond the reach of our children splashing on the shore. But they too are getting old enough to swim out and join us in talk, comfortable even in fresh water.

When we go to visit my mom, who now lives right at the ocean's edge, I laugh as my children make disgusted faces at the taste of salt; I laugh as they delight in its generous buoyancy, push heavy logs free with the help of the encroaching tide and ride them on the wonderful warm (well, once you get used to it!) southeasterly waves.

All of us go in with my mom, in the evening before dinner. It is ridiculous, this virtue we make of swimming. But we still stand, exhilarated and salty, shaking our heads in astonishment at the fact that although there are dozens of houses along the choice waterfront, the beach is empty. And later, my mom, still in her bathing suit, stands dripping on a towel in the kitchen, mashing the potatoes that boiled while we swam. For a moment, the quiet clutch of fear that underscores all the pleasures of spawning children relaxes in the aftermath of ritual in my mom's house beside the ocean.

Liz McKenna

Liz McKenna was born in Edinburgh, Scotland and lived in various places across Canada from Newfoundland to Prince Rupert where she lived for over six years. Liz McKenna died in 1987.

The first day of school and for many days afterwards, "Teacher says" was Christopher's favourite way to start a sentence. "I have to brush my teeth after meals." This last request was very hard on toothpaste. Some of it always ended up on the floor, on his sweater, or if it was mint flavoured, just swallowed.

In the mornings, he was in such a hurry to go to school he wouldn't eat breakfast. Soon the refrigerator was covered with his paintings. The pictures were usually of his father or me and were very uncomplimentary. I asked him a few times to bring a painting of his teacher home. He'd talked so much about her, all complimentary — I found myself wanting to meet this paragon who was stealing my son's affections.

After a few weeks, an invitation came to attend a parents' meeting at the school. Christopher was so excited — now he could show us HIS teacher. We were excited too, and slightly apprehensive about his progress in the three 'R's.

Unfortunately our progress into the classroom was halted by a large poster at the entrance.

Each pupil's first name was on the poster in alphabetical order and across the top in big print was "What I have for breakfast." I saw the teacher too. Surely there was a smirk on her very homely face. I started at the top of the list. Alan had milk and cereal. Brian had sugar puffs and orange juice. Celeste had French pancakes, maple syrup, bacon and eggs, orange juice, coffee and jelly beans. I thought Celeste had a great future ahead of her, as a writer of fairy tales.

The next name was Christopher. A large NOTHING filled the allocated space. My husband, seeing my shocked look said, "At least he's truthful."

I moaned, "I wish he had Celeste's imagination."

Maybe I wished too hard. About three months later, we were invited to an Open House night at the school. A young teacher's aide was stationed at the classroom door. She asked us our name. We told her. She said "Ah, you must be Christopher's parents. It's a pleasure to meet a father who takes his son with him on hunting trips. I like to see a strong bond between father and son."

I didn't see my husband's face. My own was buried in my coat collar. I hurriedly backed out of the classroom before I exploded with laughter: my husband who catches a fly in a tissue, then opens the window to free it.

I wasn't surprised at year's end to see on Christopher's report card the comment, "Your son has a vivid imagination." I'd already found out that Celeste had been seated next to him in class for a month.

Iain Lawrence

Mama was in the kitchen, cutting heart-shaped cookies from a slab of dough, when we got the news that Peter had drowned at sea.

I think she knew, the minute the phone rang. The cookie cutter slid across the dough, digging little furrows and scratching at the wood underneath. Mama dusted her hands on her apron and reached for the phone. A cloud of flour swirled above the table and settled toward the floor.

"Hello," she said. Softly.

Mama didn't speak after that. She just listened. She turned to face the window, looking out to the sea. And she slowly collapsed against the glass, first her arm, her shoulder, and then her cheek. I could hear the window pane crackling in its frame.

When she hung up the phone, there was a white handprint, like a skeleton palm, on the receiver.

"He's gone," she said. "Peter."

"Gone?" I said.

Mama dug the cookie cutter out of the dough, folded the tattered mass twice, and sprinkled it with flour. She put all her weight on the rolling pin, spreading the thick dough in every direction.

When she spoke, her voice was like water dripping from a faucet. "He fell overboard," she said, pushing with each word at the rolling pin. "They saw him go. He looked back at them when he fell. He shouted."

Mama picked up the cookie cutter, started pressing out the little hearts. "They turned the boat around," she said. "But he was gone."

Peter. My little brother. He'd left so happily a week before, all his clothes stuffed into a canvas bag. Fishing with his dad. And his boots, my boots. Steel toes, two sizes too big. Dragged him down.

"Oh, mama," I said. My throat felt raw and sore.

Mama shook a wilting heart from the cookie cutter, set it down, and crouched on the floor beside my chair.

"Don't cry," she said, putting her arms around my waist. "Please don't cry."

Mama was smiling, but her eyes were grey and dull. She reached up and placed a cold hand against my cheek.

"You were making these cookies for him," I said. "Weren't you?"

"Yes." She stood, hugged my head firmly against her apron, smelling of flour. "He'll be hungry when he comes home."

I looked up, saw Mama silhouetted in the window. The morning light shone in her hair, splashed down over her shoulder. Her face was black, shapeless, but a tiny glint shone from her eyes. And she was humming to herself.

Mama was still humming, a cracked and tuneless sound, as she took the cookies hot from the oven and packed them into a paper bag. She left through the back door, heading down the walkway to the beach.

I watched her descend the rocks, balancing awkwardly on the boulders, her arms held out girlishly for balance. She settled herself down among the exposed roots of an old cedar tree that leaned out over the water. When we were younger, Peter and I swung on a rope tied to a limb of that tree.

Peter's initials were carved into the bark. I could see them as I walked down an hour later. PW + JM. He'd used an X-Acto knife to whittle them out. When he swung down from the branch, hanging upside down, the knife had fallen out of his pocket and stuck in his cheek. Two stitches, and he still had the scar, a thin white line on his face.

"Mama," I said.

She was leaning against the tree, her head on the rough bark. The bag of cookies sat beside her, its top rolled tightly down. There was a brown butter stain on the bottom of the bag.

"Mama. Come back to the house."

"He's coming home," she said, looking quickly in my direction then turning back, out to sea. "I want to be here when he comes."

"Where was dad?" I said. "When'll he be in?"

"Two days," she said. "Tomorrow night, maybe."

"Come back to the house, Mama."

She shook her head. I sat beside her, feeling the cold roughness of the stone through my trousers.

"Do you remember," she said, "when Oyster died?"

I nodded. Peter's kitten. A little white thing, it had simply collapsed one day. One minute it was chasing a ball of wool across the floor. The next minute it was dead, grotesquely, its lips curled back and its eyes open. Peter was about five, then.

"Remember what Peter said?"

"No."

"He came running to me with Oyster in his arms, still warm and floppy, and asked me what was wrong with it."

And you picked it up," I said, remembering. "And you looked at it, and said it was dead."

Mama had closed the kitten's eyes and pinched its lips into place. "It's dead," she'd told him. And Peter, who was crying, had looked up at Mama and said, "For how long?"

I moved closer against the tree until my shoulder was touching Mama's.

"Oyster didn't come back," I said.

Mama only looked at me. A few minutes later, I walked slowly back to the house.

Mama never moved all morning. She stayed by the tree as the sun swung around to the west, as still as the stones. Occasionally she reached up to brush a strand of hair from her eyes. A dozen times, I trudged back and forth to the beach.

"He's coming," was all she said.

I watched the sun set through the kitchen window, then stood in the darkened room until the water turned to black and the tree faded into the night. I rolled up a blanket and carried it down to the beach.

Come inside, Mama," I said. "Come and wait in the house."

"I want to be here," she said. The plate of sandwiches I'd brought her earlier, the thermos of honey-sweetened tea, hadn't been touched. "A while ago, I heard him calling to me."

I shook the blanket open and arranged it over Mama's legs, tucking it up to her shoulders. "You're cold," I said.

"No," she said. "I'm not. But thank you."

"I'll wait with you," I said, and sat down again beside the tree. A red running light passed on the water. A moment later I heard the rumble of an engine and, long after, the wake washed against the shore below us.

"Tide's turned," said Mama. "He'll come on the rising tide."

I fell asleep, there beside the tree, and dreamt of Peter. I saw him come staggering out of the water, strands of kelp wrapped around his arms and his legs, trailing behind him on the mud. I heard the water squelching in his boots and saw that big coat of his billowing back from a bloated body, a hideous smile on his puffed, white face.

When I woke up, it was Mama that was screaming.

"It's Peter," she shrieked. She was on her feet, pointing down to the water, the blanket piled around her ankles. "He's coming home."

It was dawn. A deep, dark red dawn. Sailors take warning, I thought automatically, following Mama's pointing arm to a dark shape on the edge of the mud. It was rocking back and forth in the wavelets.

Mama scrambled down the beach and ran laughing through the mud, leaving behind her a weaving line of huge, black-edged footmarks.

"It's a log, Mama," I cried. "It's just a log. Oh, God, Mama."

She'd trod on her bag of cookies, splitting the paper and knocking it down between the stones. I set it back by the tree, hearing crumbs rattle inside, and picked my way across the rocks.

Mama was lying in the mud and water, her arms draped around the rotting driftwood. Thick ooze clotted in her hair and gobs of it had fallen off where her head rested on the wood. She was sobbing desperately.

"I thought it was him," she said. "I was sure it was him."

"He's not coming home, Mama," I said.

She cried against the wood and the log heaved with her, rising and falling in the water, bumping gently on the bottom. The tide was rising.

"Come back to the house," I said.

I crouched down, plucked Mama's hands from the wood. She clutched them to my shoulders and pressed her face against my shirt. The mud was cold and reeked of decay.

"Dad'll be home soon." I said.

We sank to our knees in the mud as we struggled together toward the rocks. Halfway there, Mama stopped, her hands tearing at my clothes.

"Did you hear it?" she said, looking up with eyes that reflected the red of the sky. It was starting to rain. "Peter's out there. He's coming now."

"No, Mama," I said.

"But I heard him." Her eyes were wide, pleading. "I heard him calling to me."

"It was only seagulls."

We trudged through the mud, feeling it gradually harden under our feet, and started up the rocks toward the tree. There were still a few strands of blue rope tied to an upper limb.

I picked up the blanket as we passed, dragged it under one arm.

Later, when Mama finally fell asleep, her mud-crusted hair staining the back of her armchair, I went back for the sandwiches and thermos. Ravens had ripped open the paper bag and scattered scraps of paper, bits of cookies, across the beach. They rose in a squawking black cloud and settled in the branches of the tree.

I picked up the largest fragments of Mama's cookies, broken hearts lodged between the rocks, and gently cast them out over the water.

For Peter.

Joan Skogan

Marine Insurance policy #12-94160
for the fishing vessel
JOANNA C.
is an unexpectedly
tender document.
The assurers, it says,
"are contented to bear
and do take upon us . . .
the adventures and perils
of the sea,"
including:
"men of war, fire, theft,
enemies and pirates."
Also,
"rovers, thieves, jettisons,
surprisals, takings at sea,
arrests, restraints,
and other losses
and misfortunes."
This policy,
which also provides for
"a port of refuge,"
applies, of course,
only to the aforementioned
vessel, and the gear
presently aboard her.

Paul McCuish

Paul McCuish lives on a small island near Queen Charlotte City, BC. His work on the Queen Charlotte Islands "gave me time for hanging around the docks and Margaret's Cafe, where they do wear their Stanfield woollies on the outside — men and women, summer and winter." He now teaches elementary children who wear what children wear anywhere else in the country, but he no longer has time for "hanging around" — or for much writing.

Peter Fletcher closed the door to Jason's bedroom, glancing at his watch to see how long the Tylenol had taken to put the child to sleep. It was wonderful stuff, he thought, as he kicked the wet flannel diaper across the hall to the bathroom. He picked up a stuffed rabbit, a yo-yo, and an armless G.I. Joe camouflaged amongst coffee stains and lint on the weathered leaf-patterned chesterfield and piled them onto a horde of other treasures in Jason's toy box, quietly, in dread of waking the child.

The old barrel stove had dried the green blocks of hemlock he'd been trying to burn all morning, and the house was finally warm. He struggled out of his gray woollen undershirt, scratching himself through the jack shirt he was wearing under it, and dug through yesterday's mail and newspapers for a magazine. He tucked it under one armpit, filled his cup from the gently perking pot of coffee on the wood stove, and collapsed happily into the comfortable green chair in the bay window.

His life at the moment could be worse, he thought. Had been worse only recently. A week ago he had been sitting at a small round table in the Legion bar, spending the last of his final U. I. cheque on beers and Cheezies and wondering how he would purchase his way home to Thunder Bay. The Queen Charlotte Islands were not the wonderland he had envisioned from the middle of a cold Ontario winter. The unspoiled wilderness and quaint communities at the edge of the world were, in fact, as cold and wet and as unwelcoming as any of the numerous places he had lived before. He hadn't seen the wilderness. There were no roads to it, and after the indignity of being flat on the deck for six hours on the crossing from Prince Rupert, he was not excited about going for another round of seasickness on one of the old fishing boats that local mariners had salvaged from the beaches to charter for tourists.

The local business community had not been impressed with his year and a half at a college of business administration, and nobody had offered him employment that was challenging enough, or that paid enough, for him to accept. And now he was broke. He had been broke before, but never so friendless and so far from home.

Julie Watson and Elizabeth Keis had been watching Peter with an interest that grew greater as they drank more and more of something that Billy behind the bar was calling a 'Gill Netter.' They had been reviewing the events leading to Julie's recent marital collapse, and lamenting Elizabeth's many years of rotten luck in relations with undeserving men, and they recognized a fellow founderer.

The young man they'd been watching seemed to be all out of beers and Cheezies and was digging unsuccessfully through all of his pockets for a means of ordering more. He was a man, which that night was not much to his credit, but he was young and nice looking and pathetic, and they thought they could pity him.

They bought him a beer and were encouraged by his boyish delight. They bought him Cheezies and he invited himself to their table. He had manners and charm and a refreshing intelligence. They were impressed that he had dropped out of his business courses in his final year of university to study philosophy. They did their best to impress him in turn.

Their conversation glossed over the state of world politics, spiralled in erratic forays against the norms of patriarchal society, bounced about the idea of new social patterns, and concluded with a commitment to establishing a higher order of morality, especially for men. When Billy announced closing time, Peter went home with them.

Peter was adept at fading into social landscape, and he adjusted himself nicely to difficulties of sharing a small space with two women and a child. He pulled up a wooden box for a chair at breakfast the next morning and helped clean up afterward. Julie and Elizabeth left for work together, taking Jason between them to leave with a sitter. Only Jason was feeling well, so only Jason had spoken. Nobody had answered.

Peter was still there when the women and Jason returned late in the day. They were surprised, but Julie and Elizabeth took advantage of his presence and went immediately to bed, leaving the baffled child to instruct Peter in the preparation of supper. Peter obliged, not questioning the nutritional value of spaghetti with brown sugar and peanut butter.

The following morning, after dropping Jason at the sitter's, Julie quizzed Elizabeth about Peter's lingering.

"Did you take him to bed?"

"God no! Did you?"

"Uh uh. So why is he still here?"

"I suppose he can't afford to leave."

"Well, send him to Social Services. I'm tired of him lurking around the house with his grinning face. He looks like Greg when he grins like that. Remember Greg?"

"Greg rooted through your underwear drawer when nobody was home."

"I think Greg was wearing my underwear when nobody was home."

"Greg was a pig."

"Peter's not so bad as that, but let's get him out."

"You sent Paul to Social Services to get him out. Jody will murder you if. . . ."

"I don't think Peter would play epilepsy in her waiting room. Jesus, Paul was such an actor. What a pig."

"You can talk to him."

"I talked to Greg and Paul."

"Peter isn't mine."

"He's half yours."

"What if he could do something useful. If he could fix things. Jesus, everything in the house that could rust or rot or break down has done it."

"He hasn't indicated a natural propensity."

"Or baby-sit. Or cook."

"Baby-sit would be wonderful. I'm tire of dragging Jason half asleep through the dark to leave him all day at Linda's. I've heard him call her 'Mom'."

"Let's suggest it to him."

"Maybe he doesn't know about kids."

"We can teach him. He looks bright, when he isn't grinning."

"We can teach him to cook."

"We can teach him to clean up, and behave like men should around women."

"Sort of make him an apprentice."

"Teach him to respect women."

"Appreciate us."

"We can make him into a good husband for somebody."

"Teach him not to cut paper with your sewing scissors. He was cutting a cardboard box up to start the stove."

"What a pig."

Peter sat happily alone in the comfortable wicker chair in the bay window, with his hands wrapped around the warm mug of coffee, wondering if his newly acquired employment would qualify him for U. I. The Charlottes had not treated him very kindly until his discovery of the two women. They seemed to appreciate him.

He felt like some sort of saviour toward them, being there to help out in so many ways, kind of like he'd been sent by some higher order of destiny or something. Man, they needed him around the place — two women with no physical skills. It must have been lonely for them, he thought, and he wondered if they were trying to figure out which of them would have him, or if they both would. Whichever way they decided would be fine; until now the islands had not accommodated him well with respect to sex, either. He wished they would decide soon, though, because he wanted to talk about money. He was doing a lot for them, but he didn't want to talk money until the sex thing was clearly worked out. This was not going to be a prostitution relationship. They had given him a hundred bucks, and he'd saved a few more from being thrifty with the money they'd given him for grocery shopping. And Julie had let him help himself to the clothes that her husband had left behind. But that wasn't enough. A man needed an income, and a room of his own would be nice. . . .

Peter had another coffee and read another magazine. God, he thought, women read such trash. Six women's magazines he'd read cover to cover and nothing worthwhile in any of them. He stretched, yawned, and got slowly up from the chair to check on Jason, worrying a bit about him sleeping so long. If he wasn't awake before Julie and Elizabeth came home, they might get on to the Tylenol thing. They were not happy about his new habit of staying awake so long in the evenings.

He prodded the child until it stirred, murmured and slumped back to sleep. It would probably wake up all right. He put water in a couple of pots and placed them on the stove. They would inspire him, by and by, with their potential for becoming something. He liked an organic process like that. He poured another coffee.

"Organic process! Bullshit."

"Julie, he won't wake up," called Elizabeth.

"God, Peter, put a potato in this one, and something green in the other one. I'll make a meat loaf. I'm coming, Liz!"

"Meat loaf? Come on, we have meat loaf all the time," he complained.

"Julie!"

"You know where to go for something different, Peter. I'm coming, Liz! Chrissakes."

"He seems fine. Just won't wake up."

"Peter says he only went down a little while ago. Says they were outside all day."

"Doing what?"

"Probably parading his new clothes around to impress the community."

"You shouldn't have given them to him."

"I didn't mean for him to take the whole works. God. What a pig."

". . . and don't call me a pig! I'm not your husband, you know."

"Oh Yeach! Liz, I've got cramps and a headache. And no Midol."

"Peter used them all?"

"Not funny, ladies!"

"We're not ladies — we're women!"

"Well, you're not ladies. . . ."

"God, he's a pig. Do we have Tylenol?"

"A whole bottle of kid's Tylenol for Jason."

"I'll try anything. You make the meat loaf, please."

Less than twenty minutes after Julie and Elizabeth had sleuthed the truth of why the Tylenol bottle was almost empty, Peter was smiling his best smile at the Thrift Shop, determined to get his fair share from the women by selling whatever clothes he had managed to get out of their shack with. He explained the deep scratches with a story about breaking up a cat fight, but the woman at the shop didn't soften toward him. She actually expected him to give her the stuff. As a compromise, he left most of the clothing and she agreed to drive him to the ferry terminal. He was happy to leave the woollen pants and plaid jack shirt and the gray Stanfield's underwear that everybody here, even the women, wore on the outside.

*   *   *

Byron Johnston's landlord had disconnected the power to his room as a prelude to evicting him, and the young man had constructed a stove out of a trash can. He dug pieces of fencing from beneath the rubble and put them carefully in the can. Flames licked up around the boards, casting a ragged shadow against the bare wall opposite. He sat before the glowing can amongst the brick and the dancing shadows, wondering how he could get enough money to get out of Rupert. To Vancouver, he thought. Or farther south — it was so bloody cold.

Every place he'd ever been was cold. He'd even married once to get warm, but that had turned cold, too. He'd never had a job that wasn't outside in the cold. God, he thought, I hate the cold. He had come to the west coast in the fall to escape another Winnipeg winter. He had heard that Vancouver was a booming city. He wasn't exactly a journeyman in any trade, but he'd worked around construction sites for almost ten years, ever since leaving high school three months before he would have graduated. He should have gone to Vancouver, he thought. He hadn't, because he had fallen asleep on the train in Prince George and missed his transfer to the other rail line. He was almost in Prince Rupert before he realized his mistake. But Rupert had been fine for a while. Until winter. Winnipeg was never so cold as Rupert in the winter when it was gray and wet and the wind blew great lumps of wet snow through the smallest holes in your rain gear. After he'd quit his job the first day that it snowed, he couldn't find another. Rupert was too small a place to quit a job unless you were on your way to someplace else. Vancouver would have been better, he thought. Vancouver was bigger. And farther south.

The fire burned low, and the room grew colder and darker under its dying glow. He had no more fencing, and it would make too much noise and take too much effort to break up the chairs. He left the cat in the apartment to spite both the cat and the landlord, and slipped quietly down three flights of steps to the street, letting himself out quickly to avoid a final confrontation with any of the neighbors to whom he might have owed money. He walked, with no sense of purpose, toward town.

He loitered in hotel lobbies and barroom doorways for as long as he could, but failed to be invited to sit and drink with any of the crowd he had been welcomed by when he'd had a U. I. cheque to share. He wandered along the streets, stopping for a while to watch a man and a woman with a stolen shopping cart collecting beer cans from garbage barrels. He turned away and walked toward the waterfront, regretting not having stayed one more night in his apartment.

He remembered waking up in the morning, this morning, in the bow of a small wooden skiff at the dock between the fish plant and Smile's Cafe. A boy was nudging him with his oar. Gently. He remembered the boy's face. There was fear in his eyes, and Byron had felt ashamed that he had frightened a boy. But there was something else. The boy was worried. That had bothered Byron all day.

The waitress nudged Byron again and set his change down on the table beside the small pile of wrinkled bills she had helped herself from. Byron put his empty glass on her tray and stretched his arm out for a full one. He thought again of the man and woman collecting beer cans in the alley. He had seen them again in the morning, asleep on discarded cardboard boxes behind the Safeway store. Their drawn, angular faces and fragile frames suggested the skeletons beneath their dirty raincoats. Byron had felt afraid. No, he thought, just disgusted — he had so much more. He was young, he'd come from a good family. . . . He had very carefully laid a large, flattened box across both of them.

The liquor store next to the Safeway had just opened and he quietly pushed their cart of cans and bottles inside and waited for the clerk to total their value. He hadn't thought again about the man and the woman, he thought instead that it wasn't fair that the young clerk in the liquor store had such an easy job, such a warm job, when it was so much harder for himself. He pocketed the money and headed towards the hotel for warmth, beer, and happiness.

Peter Fletcher stood in the doorway of the Ocean View Hotel, shaking the cold Prince Rupert rain from his insufficient jacket, feeling in the pungent odors of the old bar a welcome home. The poor weather had attracted a full house, and Peter wandered twice amongst the crowded tables before a lone drinker gesturing for beers with four large and unwashed fingers attracted his interest, and he exercised the social elegance that had always stood him in good stead when slipping into barroom introductions.

"Byron Johnston," the young man obliged, sitting up from his slouch in the chair. "Yeah. Sit down." He reached his hand warily over the empties on the table to lock knuckles in the brief struggle of precision and tenacity that marks so much of one man to another. "Yeah, have a beer. Here, this one's cold."

Peter kindly accepted the beer, gently blew the foam from its top, and drank in a manner intended to express appreciation. He ordered Cheezies to reciprocate. The two men in from the rain were soon comfortably intimate, as if they'd discovered a common lineage, and were unabashedly sharing their deepest insights.

"Yeah, I've done a bit of that myself. Worked a lot of things before I finished my business degree. Into Project Organizing now. Good field."

"I'm mostly into decorating now. It's like a practical art. Professional enough, but individual, right? Like, I don't wear suits and all. My work is what people judge me by."

"Worked on magazines a lot, it was kind of that way. Arty, but practical. Yeah. Had a few magazines I did projects on, like selecting materials, you know. God, the trash you gotta weed out to get a really good magazine off the press."

"Been doing a job with a lot of stone work. Been doing the really fine stuff myself — it's why my hands are like this. But working in stone is real honest work. Rewarding."

"Know just what you mean. Been organizing a big renovation project on the Islands. Charlottes. Got to know a lot of people there. Should go there if you like masonry work."

"Decorating, really."

"Yeah . . . Jesus, glad I'm out of there. Was living with two women."

"Really?"

"Good ladies, you know. But, God, a man can only give so much."

"Know what you mean exactly."

"Yeah. Man needs some space around him. Room to grow, you know—"

"Looking for a change, myself. How's the weather over there?"

"Pretty mild. Not L. A. or the Carolinas or anything. I been there once."

"Maybe if I get this job finished to where I can trust the other guys to wrap it up, might just take a look around over there. Just gotta brick up the chimney now, then a break would do me some good."

"I like to get around like that myself, once I get a project wrapped up. Yeah. I should give you some names if you ever get over. These women, you know, both working. And they could use a guy with skills like you've got. Maybe not decorating."

"Oh, like I do all kinds of stuff. Most trades. They got a nice bar there?"

"Yeah. Pretty good bar. Couple of pretty good bars. . . ."

Byron Johnston squeezed himself out of the tiny change room in the Thrift Shop, pulling the gray Stanfield's on over his jack shirt the way he'd seen some guys wearing them at Margaret's Cafe. He grudgingly parted with a dollar for his new clothes, deftly slipped a paperback novel from the book rack, tucked it under his shirt, and stepped out into a warm, blue Charlotte afternoon. He stood on the steps of the tiny porch, watching two women passing by. He called pleasantly to them asking where a person might find a good meal in town.

"Can you believe it," one woman said to the other, "he called himself a 'person', not a 'man'."

"Don't talk to him. He reminds me of you-know-who."

"No. They're not at all alike. God, that guy was a pig."

"He's dressed exactly like him. Same pants, same shirt. The same underwear."

"Everybody here dresses like that. He looks like he's not even from near here."

"He reminds me of home, somehow."

"Yeah. That's it."

"Some place a person could get a beer and a steak," Byron tried again.

"Legion," one woman called back. "Tonight's steak night. It's a quiet place."

"Exactly what I'm looking for. I like a quiet place."

"We're going to the Legion now, as a matter of fact," the other called to the man in the Stanfield grays.

Dene myth for the people at Moricetown, B.C.
(from Father Morice's notes)

Joan Skogan

The young hunter slept wrapped in a black bear skin, his body curved like the new moon around the circle of his fire. Frost stiffened the hides hung over the lodge entrance and the sleeper's breath clouded above him.

Pine wood snapped in the fire and in one motion the young man was on his feet staring at the night sky rounded in the roof opening over the fire. He brushed aside the door coverings and stepped into the night. Yoehta, star shape of the Great Bear, hung overhead. The bright, sharp points of Yoehta's eye stars looked down on the dark blur of the forest, on the lodge with a thread of smoke rising from its roof hole, on the dogs sleeping beside the entrance, and on the young hunter.

He looked back at the Great Bear in the sky. Yoehta had walked only half his journey across the night and though the hunter longed for morning, dawn was far off. The young man wrapped himself in the bear skin robe and slept curled around his fire. Once more he awoke suddenly and stepped outside. Old Yoehta seemed to stand as still in the heavens as the hunter who stood on earth. He threw more wood on his fire and lay down again. Behind his closed eyes, the hunt began: the trail, the dogs running beside him, the bear, sleepy and blundering in the cold, the certain arrow.

Once and once again he stepped out to see if Old Yoehta moved toward morning. The bear stars, far from their journey's end at the edge of the sky, stared down at him.

The young man cried out, "How slowly you move, Yoehta!" His voice splintered into laughter. "You are old indeed. . . ." The words faded into the cold, quiet dark. The hunter sat by his fire until the dogs stirred at first light. He called to them and set out. His feet moved lightly on the trail and his eyes flashed, seeking signs of bear, the broken branch, a print on the frosted ground. He smelled the promise of snow on the wind. Far ahead he heard his dogs barking. He ran towards them.

The dogs crouched by an old man sitting on a stump in a small clearing. His white hair lifted in the wind and his sharp, bright eyes shone from a face slashed with streaks of vermillion paint. He held a staff before him and he looked hard at the young hunter. "Come here to me," he called and the hunter came forward from the forest.

"You laughed at me," the old man said. "You cried out in the night, saying I am old and walk the sky too slowly." No breath clouded from his mouth and the hunter tried to turn away from the red-painted man with the shining eyes, but he could not. "Still," the old one continued, "each night I walk the journey you travelled this morning. And you will find that is further than you knew." The young man tried to close his ears to the these words, but he could not.

"Your way home will be long," the old man's voice went on, "and the path is not marked. Perhaps," he paused, "perhaps if you take my staff and use it as I tell you, your journey will bring you home." He held out the long spruce pole, but the young man did not reach for it. He whistled to his dogs, but they sat at the feet of the old man and even their ears did not move to his whistle. The hunter looked for his homeward trail, but the forest circled the clearing without a break. The path he travelled that morning was gone. He looked again at the old man with the red slashed cheeks and bright eyes, then he reached out and grasped the staff.

"Let no other hand touch it." the old man said. "When you fail to find game, and you will, when you hunger. and you will, stand it before you, straight between earth and sky, and let it fall. If it falls to the way of the north wind, do not go there, for famine waits that way." The young hunter looked at the spruce pole that seemed the same as any other, long and slim and strong. the wood stripped of bark and polished with handling.

The old man went on. "If it falls toward the rising or the setting sun, you will find bears, both male and female, there. If the staff lies on the south wind's path, go carefully for you will not know what waits that way."

The hunter kept his eyes on the pole between his hands. When he looked up the old man and the dogs were gone. He stood alone within the closed circle of the forest. Gripping the spruce staff tightly, he stepped forward and a path opened between the trees.

Night after night, Old Yoehta looked down on the hunter sleeping beside the path he learned anew each day. Many times the young man found no game for his fire and, belly tight with hunger, he held the staff straight between earth and sky and let it fall where it would.

Many times he travelled on a trail leading to the rising or setting sun. As the man with the painted face and shining eyes told him, male and female bears, often of shape and colour strange to him, waited for his arrows.

When he walked towards the warm south wind, he found all was new to him, Once, he went the north wind's way and lay dying from hunger until he let the stick fall beside him. The staff showed him the path and supported him as he staggered through the snow towards food and fire.

The hunter's journey and his life joined as he walked. Under the moon he slept, under the sun he walked, until ahead he saw his home, small in the distance. His footsteps were slow now, but sure and steady, and his old lodge grew larger as he walked on, still holding the spruce staff.

The roof of his lodge was broken with the weight of many snows and his house poles were leaning and grown over with moss. He set the spruce staff straight between earth and sky at the lodge entrance and cleaned the leaves and pine needles from the circle of fire stones. He made a fire and curved his body around it and slept.

The night sky covered the roofless lodge and the sleeping hunter. The wind stirred his white hair and firelight striped his cheeks red when Old Yoehta looked down on him.

Andrew Wreggitt

Poet, playwright, and screenwriter Andrew Wreggitt grew up in northern B.C. and lived three years in Prince Rupert. He is currently writing for such television programs as *North of 60* and *Destiny Ridge* as well as working on the screenplay version of the play *Wild Guys* which he co-wrote with his wife Rebecca Shaw.

"Midden, Prince Rupert Harbour" was inspired by the magic that is the North Coast.

The archeologists have found a child
1500 years old
Its tiny skull cracked by the weight
of overburden, the burial box,
a trace of decayed wood
The bones have shifted,
no cartilage or muscle to hold
the delicate symmetry

Later, the archeologists go home
to a small house on Digby Island,
plastic tacked over the windows,
moss hanging on the roof
This house also rests on a shell midden
The place they break open their canned food,
sleep, read magazines,
the same place the Tsimshian came
2,000 years before
to work and eat
and later fall asleep
in the same dark drizzle of rain
We've built our homes
over each other,
inhabit the same deep water harbour,
the same fresh water springs

We are drawing a picture
with ourselves, our buildings,
our trowels and brushes
We are devising a symmetry

It is possible to stand
above this small grave and mourn
a forgotten death
It is possible to dig in the shattered earth
and meet yourself
rising out of the sea of shells,
the broken child
who pushes up the world

Joan Skogan

"If you read it in a book, you'd never believe it," Rose's mother says when Rose tells one of her stories about something that really happened to someone she knows. Rose's stories all take place up the coast or in the north, never in Vancouver. They usually show that hard times or courage or love, or some question about all three, are on Rose's mind. The people in the stories don't fit comfortably around her mother's polished fruitwood table, scattered with sherry glasses on Sunday afternoons.

"You do it deliberately," Rose's mother will say, frowning at a bowl of pink and red tulips on the mantelpiece. "Are those tulips past it? It's probably too warm for them in here."

"Do I?" Rose asks.

For example, Rose knows a woman who lived in a floathouse in Simoom Sound, years ago, mind you, but still . . . she's cooking in a logging camp and one night her door flies open on the wind and the dark and in come two of the loggers carrying a boy. He's maybe twenty, only been in the camp a couple of days, and he's bleeding all over the floor from cuts on his neck and arm and a deep wound in his thigh. The fight doesn't matter to the story. They lay him down and he soaks her couch before she can bind him up with the first aid kit bandages.

The bandages run out, so she starts using towels and sheets and yelling at the loggers to get ice from the freezer. She uses up the ice and has to pack frozen pork roasts and most of the deer the faller shot last week alongside the boy. The bleeding from his neck slows down and his arm is okay, but blood still wells from his leg no matter how tightly she twists the sheets.

It's past midnight now and the boy is pale and hasn't said anything for a long time. The floathouse is crashing around and the wind won't drop until morning. One of the loggers is back in the bunkhouse and the other is sleeping in a chair while the woman is bent over the boy, trying to trickle sugared tea into his mouth. Her arm is propped on a pile of sheets and she is thinking, God forbid, that tomorrow is clean laundry day in the bunkhouse.

At three in the morning the boy is still. She's so tired of wrapping the top half of him with blankets while she raises his leg, then lowers it to tighten and loosen the sheet soaking with blood, that she falls asleep. For how long, she doesn't know. When she wakes, she's sure he's dead.

She jumps up and goes to the cupboard. Rose imagines her walking stiffly, looking as if she knows exactly what she's doing. She gets one of the thick, white coffee cups and goes back to the boy, unwinds the sheet stiffened and heavy with blood and reveals the wound. She presses the coffee cup into his slashed flesh and blood crawls down the side of the cup. When the bottom of the cup is covered, she ties the last sheet around the leg and goes to the stove. She fills the cup with hot water from the kettle and adds an Oxo cube.

Rose wonders if it's the combination of an ordinary Oxo cube with the mystery of the blood that makes her mother so angry when she tells her about the woman in Simoom Sound.

The woman marches — Rose always sees her marching — over to the boy she thinks is dead, or so close it doesn't matter. She tilts his head back roughly, (she said herself she wasn't gentle at this point) pinches his nose and pours what's in the cup down his throat. Most of it comes up, but some goes down. She only does it once.

The plane comes in the morning and in the hospital at Alert Bay, they pump blood into him for two days. For years after that he writes to the woman in Simoom Sound on his birthday. Rose has seen the letters. The last one came from Fort McMurray. The woman never told the boy, or anyone else until she told Rose, about the cup of blood.

Rose is satisfied with everything about this story. It all really happened. If she believes the facts of it, she has to accept the questions too. What made the woman give him his own blood and did it make any difference and why did she keep it secret? If her mother read about the woman from Simoom Sound in a short story and didn't have to believe she was real, she wouldn't mind so much, Rose thinks.

When Rose lived up the coast, her mother sent her new books once or twice a year. "So you won't get too out of touch with reality," her note might say. Or, "So you'll know what's really happening." Exclamation mark. "Love mother." The books were almost always novels and short stories about women who thought deeply about their unsatisfactory lives, then changed them.

"You read too much," her husband used to say. "It's not the real world." Meaning, Rose thinks, you feel too much and it makes for trouble. She thinks he might be right about the reading, at least. Fiction can't help her now.

Perhaps her mother thinks so too. These days she gives Rose photocopies of articles about mid-life careers and divorce settlements and suggests she should make notes. Rose rubs neatsfoot oil into her old boots for a long time before she does this.

She slides down in her chair, props her booted feet on the table and reads, "Revised divorce laws in British Columbia mean that all property accumulated during a marriage will be divided between both partners on the dissolution of the marriage." In the margin of the article she sketches a tiny seine boat complete with cabin and drum, then draws a line bisecting the boat from bow to stern. Thinks of a story, second-hand and from long ago, but she believes it. The old man who told it told to her must have been a boy when Sing got on the train with him at Hazelton sometime in the 1920s.

Sing — he was old himself, then — sits by the train window, staring out. A stretch of the Skeena River goes by while the boy wonders how far it is down the river to Prince Rupert, then he asks the old Chinese man where he's going.

A long time ago, more than fifty years ago, Sing tells him, he's in the Cariboo looking for gold. But he's too late. He hears news of gold on Manson Creek, though, far to the north. So he buys a mule and some grub and gear, an outfit, he calls it, and walks to Manson Creek.

Rose is recalling the start of this story more carefully than she usually does, (it's the end she usually concentrated on) and she frowns, knowing the old man who told her the story, and she herself, does not doubt for a moment his walking to Manson. The journey and the man who made it deserved this respect. Some people, Rose thinks, will not understand even this much about the story.

When Sing gets to Manson Creek, he finds gold. He stakes a claim and a government man named Billy Steel registers it. Winter is coming on and people tell him how cold and hard it's going to be, maybe 40 below. He cuts a lot of wood and gets through the winter, though it's just as bad as everyone says. In the spring he starts mining again and he finds it hard to work all day, then cut wood and cook.

So he walks the trail to Fort Babine. Rose can't figure this out, not on a modern map, anyway. How did he cross Takla Lake? Why not go down to Fort St. James? When she remembers this part of the story, Rose mourns briefly that she had been so close to Manson Creek and not seen it. She has been to Fort St. James, along Stuart and Trembleur Lakes and to Takla Landing, but not to Manson Creek. She knows gold was discovered on the Omineca River in 1871, though, and that Manson Creek flows into the Omineca.

At Fort Babine, Sing gets what he calls a Klooch, a Babine Indian woman called Emma. Emma is a good woman. "A damn good woman," Sing says, and the old man who told Rose the story says, and now Rose always says when she tells the story.

Emma not only cuts wood and cooks and keeps the cabin clean, she works in the mine. Sometimes she runs a trapline and packs furs into the Fort for grub.

Sing and Emma live in this way together for many years, very many years, and all is well. Then comes the winter when they are both old and there is a silence between them for days. At last Emma says, "I know you want to go to China and die." And they are silent again.

Sing goes to the bank, he says, and gets out the gold dust and nuggets and dumps them onto a buckskin. He takes a stick and divides the pile of gold in half, and Emma sews the buckskin into little bags to hold the gold for both of them.

Sing and Emma walk to Fort Babine where he leaves her, taking the other trail out to Hazelton and the train. Sing mentions the government's eternal promises to build a road instead of a trail out from the Fort, which makes the old man who tells the story laugh, and Rose too. She was on the Fort Babine road, gravelled now, at last, just last year.

Sing will take the Union steamship from Prince Rupert to Victoria, then an Empress boat to China. The boy listening to his story has two questions. "Was Emma really your wife?" he says.

Sing answers, "When you live fifty years in the same house with a good woman, that's a wife, even if there was no preacher."

When the boy asks, "Was there really a bank up there?" Sing laughs.

"I dug a hole in the bank when I first came to Manson Creek. Covered it with mud and brush and no one finds it in fifty years.

"You believe everything you want to believe," Rose's husband said when she told him Sing and Emma's story. No, Rose thinks, she doesn't believe everything she wants to believe. Not anymore. But she believes the story about Manson Creek.

Rose decides not to tell this story to her mother no matter how desperate she feels on a Sunday afternoon. She would be upset to know Rose is remembering Sing and Emma, managing the end of their life together with sorrow and grace, instead of thinking about her own property settlement. Her mother would be angered by the story too, for reasons Rose no longer expects to understand.

Does she have a story her mother will want to believe, Rose wonders while she's folding the divorce article into a coaster and filling the kettle for tea. Her third cup of tea is cold before she remembers the silver bracelet.

Elizabeth has worn the bracelet on her left arm for seventy years, and her mother wore it before that. It shines softly against the blurred blue flowers on the tablecloth and chimes on the teapot when Elizabeth fills Rose's cup. The inner curve of the bracelet is dented and the wings of the eagle carving are nearly worn away.

Elizabeth is twelve, going to work in the cannery for the first time, the summer her mother gives her the bracelet. Rose imagines her, small and straight-backed, sitting in an open boat with the others from the village, crossing the Skeena at slack water. Her right hand is curved over the bracelet.

When the season is over and the salmon are done, Eddie comes to take Elizabeth to Port Simpson to help with her aunt's new baby. The wind blows strong southeast off Jap Point and Eddie's little boat rolls wildly. Elizabeth leans out to re-fasten the wheelhouse door, stumbles, then slides down the narrow, tilted deck and partially into the sea. The bracelet, loose on the thin arm, catches on a cleat, holds long enough for Eddie to sweep her back.

Her shoulder is wrenched and still gives her trouble. There's a lot of snow and a long winter in Port Simpson, but Christmas is a good time with all the singing; and the baby, a boy, gets fat. It's a flat calm all the way to Prince Rupert and up the river when Eddie takes Elizabeth back to her mother at Easter.

Rose has lost the silver bracelet story for so long that it doesn't seem familiar to her now. But, like the story of the woman in Simoom Sound, and Sing and Emma's story, like Rose at her mother's table remembering other places and other people, the story of Elizabeth and the bracelet her mother gave her is true. Rose thinks her mother will believe this story, and will want her to believe it too.

Joanna M. Weston

Born in England, Joanna Weston has lived on northern Vancouver Island for over fifteen years. Her poetry has appeared in a variety of magazines.

the land took flight
thousand-winged in lift

sea burst upward
as a surge of birds

land and sea meshed
in the beat of wings

converting sky
to updraft of sound

Kenneth Campbell

Kenneth Campbell is a Prince Rupert writer. He has published numerous non-fiction articles about North Coast history. His recent non-fiction book is *North Coast Odyssey: the Inside Passage from Port Hardy to Prince Rupert.*

Ten thousand years before, a glacier had carved its graffiti into the Pacific coast, gouging a channel, straight as the path of the south-easterly winds. Now a tug headed north through the passage, pulling a barge stacked with mobile homes. They were packed three tiers deep, like shoe boxes.

Off the channel, protected from the south-easters, was a harbour which held the remnants of a community. At the bay's head stood a venerable dock; pilings remained rooted in the ocean's floor. The grayed and mossy planks clung to the pilings. And beyond the dock, the fallen shells of once-upon-a-time buildings: the cookhouse, the timekeeper's office, bunkhouses, the machine shop. The houses, too, had since collapsed, and their planks and shingles were piled in vaguely rectangular heaps that dotted the shoreline. The homes of a hundred souls who had since collapsed themselves and who lay in vaguely rectangular heaps dotting grassy fields far from the harbour.

The air was still in that desolate camp; only the silent sounds of lapping waves and the hush of the trees. Then the far-off murmur of the tug's diesel engines drifted into the bay. A solitary human, standing amid the fallen timbers, looked up. He scowled as the ship cruised past his window on the world, the harbour mouth.

"Imagine living in traps like those." He spit through his white beard.

The floating pile of people-boxes drifted out of sight. The old man moved on further, stepping over roof boards studded with rusty nails. Once he had lived under this wood. With his boot, he stirred the rotting wood; the memories and the ghosts came rushing out at him. The sounds of the camp rang out once more: caulk boots on the wooden floor, the crack of axe striking wood, the satisfied scraping back of chairs after a cookhouse meal.

And the music. When they pushed back the tables on a Saturday night and the whole camp packed in for the dance — single men, couples and their kids, even the teachers. Anyone who had an instrument brought it along, but Inky was always there with the squeeze box and the boss with his banjo. And the boots stomped and cavorted, did the bush polka, until the old cookhouse rocked on its piling foundation.

A speedboat skidded around the point into the harbour. The old man gave a wave and walked toward the float. A young man hopped out of the boat and whipped a rope around a cleat. He held out a package wrapped in a green garbage bag.

"Hiya, Frank. Here's a couple of salmon for you and Jessie. And your mail." He reached into his coat and pulled out a flimsy pile of envelopes.

Frank took the fish and the mail. "I'll give them to Jessie. What's new in the village?"

"Not much. Everybody's fishing now. Couple of university types came in on the same plane as the mail. They're staying the summer, by the sounds of it. I guess we're under the microscope again."

Frank spit into the water. "We had some archaeologists up here one time — said there was an old Indian village in the bay here. Everything was so organized, all marked off into little squares. And they dug down inch by inch, hoping to find some remains. Every little thing they found, they put into a bag, labelled it and shipped it off to the laboratory. Jesus, I had to laugh, though, because here were these guys, varsity scholars, sifting through somebody else's garbage." And he spit again.

Pete climbed into his speed boat. "Well, my people have interesting garbage, I guess," Pete said. "Just wait until they dig up the white man's garbage. They won't know what to think of some of the things they'll find."

"Crazy, the whole lot of them," the old man said as he bent over to untie the line. "Won't be any of them left to do the digging, the way they live in the cities. They'll kill themselves off and all that will be left will be guys like us who belong to the land."

"Yeah, well right now, I belong to the sea, and I better get to it. See you." Pete turned the key and the outboard drowned out Frank's goodbye.

The wash from the boat rocked the float, and Frank waited for the motion to subside before heading back up the gangplank. As he walked up the boardwalk to the log house, the smell of freshly baked bread greeted him. Jessie's round face turned to him when he swung open the door.

"Who was here?"

"Pete. He brought these." Frank untied the garbage bag and pulled out two red sockeye salmon. "And the mail." He tossed the letters on the table.

Jessie wiped her doughy hands on an apron stained by years of baking. She grabbed the letters, squinting at the addresses. "Only three. Nobody knows we're out here any more." She searched a cluttered shelf for her glasses.

Frank sliced into a steaming loaf of bread. "Anyone who knew us is long gone. All the old loggers are dead."

"One from the church," Jessie said after ripping open the largest of the envelopes. "The mission ship will be around in a month to see us."

Frank started to spit, but a quick motion of Jessie's head stopped him.

"Cut that out. You know you enjoy it when they drop in. You're just too stubborn to admit it."

He said nothing, but concentrated on buttering the bread. Jessie opened the next envelope, and read the letter in silence.

"Bertha passed away. Her daughter wrote, thought I'd like to know. That was nice of her."

Frank went to the cooler, looking for jam. "Should have stayed here. The city killed her."

"Nonsense. She's a good deal older than I." She placed the letter on the table, and took the last one. "This one's from Janie. At least we have a daughter to write to us."

Frank came back to the table with a jar of huckleberry jam and began spreading it on the bread. He bit into it while his wife read. He finished that slice and was working on another before Jessie put down the letter.

"She's sending Darren out to spend the summer with us."

"Nice of her to ask us."

"Well, it sounds like she's at her wit's end. He was expelled from two different schools this year. He can't get a job and just hangs around with bums. His father won't take him. She couldn't wait for a reply from us, so she's putting him on a plane next weekend."

"What's a city kid going to do in a place like this?"

The day the boy arrived, rain pelted the earth. Frank swore the airplane would never fly on such a day. But just after noon, the yellow Beaver circled the harbour. The old couple ran outside at the snarl of its engine and watched as it wobbled lower to the water of the channel. The floats touched down, then bucked the waves from the south-easterly winds. By the time it had taxied to the dock, Frank and Jessie were there to welcome their grandson.

The boy stared ahead as he waited for the pilot, who climbed out of the cockpit and secured the airplane to the cleat. He unlatched the passenger door and the boy stepped onto the narrow treads of the ladder that lead to the pontoon.

"Here's your grandson, safe and sound," said the pilot. "He's a pretty tough kid — a good flyer in this rough weather." He punched the boy's shoulder, then climbed into the plane to pass out boxes of groceries and an old blue suitcase.

Darren took the boxes from the pilot. He didn't look at his grandparents.

"Where did these groceries come from?" Jessie asked.

"Your daughter must have sent the money up," the pilot said. "A delivery truck brought them to the seaplane base."

Frank took the boxes from the boy, piling them in neat stacks. He put an orange plastic tarp over them to keep out the rain.

When they were done, the pilot untied the rope from the cleat, climbed in the cockpit, and waved goodbye. The boy stood watching, his eyes fixed on the airplane as it revved its motor and headed towards the opening of the bay. He let the backwash rush of wind from the propeller, the pungent oil-smelling blast of air, flow over him.

Jessie and Frank turned back from the wind and the smell and the noise of the airplane. They lifted boxes from beneath the tarp and carried them up the steep slope of the gangplank. Frank arranged them efficiently into a wheelbarrow. He turned back down the gangplank to collect the rest of the groceries, but met the boy coming up with the last of the boxes. The boy looked at his feet, awkward on the slippery wood. Frank hunched back against the railing, letting him pass.

Frank moved back up the gangplank. He grabbed the wooden handles of the wheelbarrow. The three of them — grandfather, grandmother and grandson — walked up the boardwalk, silent, through the dashing rain.

After a week the boy had said nothing. He ate voraciously, every meal, then left the house to wander. He roamed the beaches, the animal trails through the forest.

"Darren never brings back souvenirs from his walks," Jessie said one morning as she washed up the breakfast dishes. "When I'm out for a walk, I always find a curious piece of driftwood or a funny rock, even after all my years in this place."

"That's the city in him. He doesn't fit in here." Frank finished the last of his morning coffee. "I'm going out to file the teeth on the chainsaw. Haven't cleaned it up for months."

In the evenings, the boy liked to chop wood. Jessie watched him from her window, watched as the summer sun lingered low in the sky, sending tree shadows across the clearing where the chopping block stood. He attacked each bolt of cedar with a fury, swinging the axe high in the air, shoulders driving it down again, cleaving the wood with a loud cracking.

A memory was triggered. Watching Frank out the teacherage window, all those years ago. What a fury he was, chopping wood, chips flying, axe flashing in the morning sun. And once he caught her watching, turned his head at an angle towards the window. She blushed and stepped back into the shadows. Bertha giggled at her. But at the next dance in the cookhouse he tentatively asked her to dance. On the dance floor, as the boys played a slow song, she circled her arms around his shoulders.

Frank sat on his handmade stool, sharpening the axe with a whetstone. Jessie was talking, trying to draw out the boy, but carrying the conversation for the three of them.

"We never wandered, your grandpa and I. We landed here, joined together, and here we stayed."

She brushed a lock of gray hair from her forehead. The boy stared at the hypnotic rhythms of stone on steel.

"I came to teach school, when the camp was big in here. Sometimes I had fifteen kids, sometimes twenty-five. All grades, too, up to eight."

The boy asked no questions, didn't want to know how they met or where his mother was born or why they stayed. Just watched his grandfather hone the blade.

Then the chore was done. Frank stretched.

"There. That'll do for tomorrow. You've chopped up all the logs I brought in. Almost our whole winter supply you've got piled up there."

The boy stood up, rinsed his coffee cup in the pail of water standing in the sink, and headed towards the loft and his bed.

"Tell you what, Darren. How about going up the hill with me tomorrow. I'll show you how to fall a tree. A good-sized one that you can chop the hell out of."

The morning sun broke with a fury, a rare, blue-rich day. The man and boy sweated as they climbed up the hill, pushing through bracken and salmonberry branches. Frank showed him some fresh bear tracks.

"After the berries. Good thing I brought along the shotgun, just to be on the safe side."

They reached a clearing and looked back at their route. The bay lay rippling at the base of the hill, a blue steel shimmer. The log house sat wedged between the forest and the sea.

Frank walked along the edge of the clearing, looking up at the cedar crowns. The boy followed, carrying the chainsaw.

"Somewhere here there's a tree I picked out long ago. Saved for a special day." Then he spied it, and quickened his pace. "Come on!"

He yanked the cord on the chainsaw. It snarled to life, cleaving the air with a loud cracking. The boy jumped back at the sound. Frank grinned, and raised the whirring teeth towards the tree.

The boy watched as his grandfather showed him how to make the cuts, angling in on the downhill side first. He stood away from the sawdust spewing from the machine. He followed his grandfather, staying behind him, protected, as the old logger stepped back and made the final slice. Then, above the saw's racket, he heard a rumbling.

"Tim-ber!" Frank cried as the tree began to lurch, more as a ritual than with any practical purpose, for they were the only two who could hear the call. "Timber!" And the trunk hit the earth, a giant flurry swishing as the crown of boughs caught the air, lifted up with the impact and staggered to a stop.

He told the boy of an accident, years ago. A kid, green, didn't hear or perhaps heed the warning cry. The falling tree hit another, ripping off a branch, sending it flying like a bullet.

"We called them sidewinders. You always got to be on the look-out for sidewinders, Darren. Them branches can break off and fly out at you. Kill you, they will."

The sidewinder had hit the kid, dropping him to the earth, a tiny flurry swishing as his body lifted up with the impact and staggered to a stop. Then seven shrill calls from the steam whistle, telling the wives at camp of the tragedy. And again, "Timber!" Another trunk fell.

"Your turn, Darren." Frank held out the chainsaw, still alive and spitting. He helped the boy as he took it tentatively.

"That's it. Support it with your shoulders. Now try this tree over here. It's not too big. Remember what I showed you."

He felt the saw teeth bite into the wood. The saw wrestled with him, whining.

"Don't fight it. Control it, but let the teeth do the work."

He braced himself with his legs, then directed the blade in a quivering line. He let the oily, cedar-sharp blast of air flow over him. The top cut was straighter, and the wedge of cedar dropped cleanly to the ground. He moved around to the back and made the final cut.

"Timber!" Frank hollered, laughing. And the second tree dropped beside the first with a shudder. Darren gave back the saw, looking straight into his grandfather's eyes.

Two days later Frank is helping Jessie with her canning. After she fills each tin with salmon, he cranks it through the old canning machine, bonding the top to the body.

"Just about done?"

"Yup. There should be enough for two more tins, I hope. That'll make four cases. I'll have to be sure to give Pete some of my jam when I jar the huckleberries."

A howl. A snarl through the window. Heads jerk up. Eyes look up to the top of the hill.

The tree sways as they look up. The boy stands, shoulders back, head up to the sky.

And his voice rises over the buzz of the saw, the crashing of the tree. The call flies down the hill and echoes across the bay.

"Timber!" the boy shouts. And again, with a fury, "Tim-ber!"

Jenny Nelson

Jenny Nelson grew up in Fergus, Ontario before moving to Masset, B.C. As well as her writing, Ms Nelson is interested in the historical and environmental aspects of the Haida Gwaii/Queen Charlotte Island, and crafts. She has developed an ecological kit for the local schools. Her writing has appeared in a variety of publications including *West Coast Rhymes* (Gage Educational Publishing).

"Gwaii Haanas" was inspired by a trip to Burnaby Narrows in Gwaii Haanas, then known as South Moresby. A campaign to preserve the area has resulted in the island being managed equally by the Haida nation and the federal parks department.

> When I grow up, my father says,
> the Big Trees will be gone.
>
> I want to see the trees
> my father's seen.
>
> I want to travel on the water
> watch the otter
> slide into the sea.
> I want to see how small I am
> beside old Cedar Tree.
> I want to see the things
> that Chini's seen.
>
> I want to know the forest
> through my toes, as my foot goes,
> on moss, on beach, on rock,
> on rotting wood.
> I want to feel the forest
> with my eyes and hands and nose,
> wet clothes,
> sounds of tree-bird,

sounds of silence,
smell of mushroom, smell of cedar,
following the creeks that run
red and quiet,
water falls.
The forest calls.

I have a need
to see the Trees.
My father's seen.
Leave some for me.

N. J. Kerby

"Josephine" was inspired by the northwest B.C. area and some of its residents.

Old man lying by the hospital window
watching wrappers blow down the road.

Damn Doctors. Damn hospital. Damn brittle bones.
Damn bad luck to turn too late.
It struck him, swept him downslope, the
avalanche, with boiling fingers reaching through
the forest crushing him rolling him
throwing him to the edge of a devil's
igloo spiked with jagged, splintered wood.

He crawled pain by pain dragging his smashed leg
and his will to live down to the railroad tracks
lying there waiting for the freighter lying
there watching his tomorrows form pools of blood
about his head.

      God! Chris! what happened?
Hang on, old man,
we'll get you help George bring water oh
God, what a mess —

fog swirling fog curling no beginning no
ending deep echoes deep River's
throb throb throb
from the hill he could see the brown swollen waters
tearing twisting ripping trees and rocks out of
the banks sweeping the small canoe into the
torrent turning it round and round in

a frenzied dance with bobbing broken wood the
rushing River roaring through the rocks River —

Damn brittle bones, why won't you heal?
Spring comes I'll die
behind these frozen walls the River rushing
River rolling River grinding through the rocks River —

Mr. Olssen. Please! The Doctor would like to
talk to you

You come again, young man how I envy your youth
tall and strong you are
not old enough to bear a calloused heart like the
others
I see a light of kindness in your eyes but the
years will pass for you too and the light will become as
cold and crisp as the stocks in your safety deposit box.

Good morning, Mr. Olssen! How are you today?
Your leg does not seem to be healing as quickly
as we hoped I have reviewed your
case
and feel it best to move you to our extended
care unit at Mountain Vista Lodge —

His best friend, Hick Smith, had gone there sentenced
by the family after kidneys grew weak
he had gone to visit worn his only suit but the grey
ghost in the wheelchair was not the man
who had slid down the snowfields laughing
as he neared the precipice his packsack full
of rocks and rainbows.

I will not die like a wolf in a cage
reply as soft and strong as the River slipping
over the ebony rocks.

nurse's mouth laughed at an old man's
vain comparison.

    Bones take a while to heal
the doctor
spoke down to the form on the bed
you will get the best of attention there will be
lots of company for you to tell stories to why you
most likely know most of the residents at the Lodge already

No, he did not know anyone
they who spent their years in the town wearing soft shoes and
buying gadgets to do what two strong hands could do instead they
would not remember the silent man with his
dog and pack walking out of the past and the forest
into their town to buy a few supplies

Stubborn Norwegian the trader had said when
he refused to sell his furs for starvation
prices
stubborn enough to stay in the hills long after
the others had died or slipped away to easier lives

The old man struggled to sit up in bed his eyes
as blue as high mountain ice.
    I am going back to my cabin, he said,
    It is time to plant my potatoes

KERBY

It is unlikely, Mr. Olssen, that you will ever
walk again we must continue your care

Rush River roll River ranting
through the rocks River

I have written to my sons and they will come for me

Now, everyone knew that Chris Olssen had never
married an eccentric prospector and trapper he lived
where the river races through the canyon narrows
and Josephine Creek falls in silver mists over
the glistening walls

Poor old goat, the doctor thought as he walked away too
many of these old bachelors — no money no friends just
left with their fantasies

I have come for my Grandfather

They peered at the young man wearing a wolf
crest wool sweater brushing the swath of black hair back
from his eyes
hello, Grandfather, we just received your letter I
came

Ah, Josephine, like the ocean you were beautiful,
dark eyes that laughed with the
joy of the morning sun
upon the rolling waves
Standing on the wharf in your mission dress,
clutching a faded bonnet,
I can not marry you, Christian Olssen,

for if I do, the Whiteman's laws
will deny my children their
status.
I can not forget my people —
we are so few now.
I will not marry you, Christian Olssen,
but in the eyes of my people
we will be one.

And so they rode the Whiteman's steaming train
back up the River,
the River that forever had been the soul of her people,
back to the cabin in the cove by the canyon,
back to the totem poles rotting on the rocks above.

Ja, Josephine, your children were strong,
tall and straight like the cedar trees on
the steep mountain slopes.
And you taught them to speak the words
of your people,
and you raised them in the ways of the River.
But, Josephine, you raised our children for your people.
When you died — oh, dear God,
and when the flood and tangled salmon nets
swept your canoe into the canyon,
I could not keep the boys for myself.
They too followed the River to the ocean.
Your brothers raised them as their own.
It was better that — the townspeople
would never have accepted the children
of a mountain man.

But, God, it broke my heart.
We buried you, Josephine, amongst the tumbled rocks
where the bones of your ancestors lie
safe in unknown caves,
the forest, guardian of
your mossy grave.

The years rushed by, Josephine,
Like the River through the canyon walls.
The land changed. You would not know it now.
On the other side of the valley, they built a road.
I watched the forest melt away
And the great trucks carrying the trees to the town.
They came, Josephine,
with dollars for the timber on our land.
I sold our paradise to buy the boys
A trawler — they and the salmon have done well.
A tear for the forest, Josephine,
A tear for the trees.
Only stumps and storm-washed soil are left.
The wolves moved on to higher ground.

That was years ago. I did not bother the boys
with the presence of a lost father.
Yet they remembered, Josephine, for
one bright summer morning, when
Josephine Creek bubbled and burbled with the melting snows
he came to the cabin door —
Isaac, our grandson, son of Ben the eldest boy
saying only I have come to learn, Grandfather.
A boy of sixteen with the mind of a man I taught
him the ways of the mountains.
When he leaves school, Josephine,

he will walk the paths that you walked
a man of furs and smoked salmon.

the river now only a thread between the trees shone silver
still rushing rolling through the rocks his hand
clutching his chest exploding the canoe turned
tipped he ran screaming — Josephine! Josephine!
Jos-se-phine!

Ja.
I will sell you my timber,
Your price is fair.
All except the northeast corner.
My wife is buried there.

BURYING HUGH

Marylou Fritch

Marylou Fritch lived for fourteen years in the far north of British Columbia. Since 1989 she has lived in Prince Rupert with her husband and two children. A teacher, Marylou has written many report cards.

We discovered that Hugh had died when we met the Highway Department backhoe on our way into town that morning The car slewed a bit in the gravel as we stopped to talk with the operator, our neighbour, Frank. "Last night," he confirmed. "Thought I'd head out that way to help with the digging. Funeral's tomorrow."

For the last ten years, the Camerons had lived on their rundown ranch twenty miles from town. Hugh and his wife and kids showed up late one summer from someplace in the Prairies, with only what they could haul in a pickup truck and a battered trailer. He raised six kids and some horses on the money he earned driving a truck for Highways. The house was old, and you could see light through the walls in a few places But, with two wood stoves and enough kids and energy to split the firewood, they'd kept warm enough through the northern winters.

As is the way in isolated places, everyone had known Hugh. His neighbours and a few of his co-workers had visited him sometimes, but he was irascible and more than a bit bigoted and he couldn't count many friends. Nonetheless, the locals had noticed the courage with which he faced his drawn-out dying and the way he'd been willing to exchange pain for the right to die in his own bed. It was with respect that they drove out to the funeral Thursday afternoon.

The grave was situated next to a tool shed, about thirty feet in from the road and alongside the driveway. It was nice and flat there, and the family was able to sit on chairs placed along the far side. The gravelly soil was piled on top of some stumps at the head and foot of the opening, and the hundred or so mourners stood in a mass facing the family across the grave.

Our local preacher was an earnest young man, and he shifted uncomfortably from foot to foot as the last people arrived in their pickup trucks and parked by the corral. Hugh was not a religious man and the preacher hadn't known him except to say "Hello," but he gamely began the service with a hymn. Perhaps he felt he couldn't associate himself before God with Hugh, or perhaps he worried that reminders of

Heaven and Hell could only lead to disquieting conclusions concerning Hugh, for the young preacher passed up the chance to preach a sermon. Instead, he drew a typed paper from his pocket and read the statistics of Hugh's fifty-six years. Born, married, moves, births, death . . . that was all.

When he finished, Hugh's two grown sons and a couple of sons-in-law lowered the coffin into the ground. Then the rest of the family stood up, and they all walked into the house. In threes and fives, most of the congregation wandered to the ranchhouse until all that were left were some of Hugh's fellow roadworkers and his neighbours from down the river road. It had taken less than ten minutes.

We waited for several long minutes, the twenty or so people who had worked and lived near him. It occurred to me that as little as we liked Hugh, these were the people who knew him best, after his family. Shuffling, we looked uncomfortably at the grave and at each other. Everyone else was inside, but a feeling of incompleteness seemed to keep us there at the edge of that hole. Finally, two of the men turned, went into the shed, and rummaged around. They returned with a couple of shovels and each dropped a shovelful of dirt into the grave. Another man walked to his truck and came back with a steel snow scoop, and someone found a spade by the garden. Picking up rhythm, they began to fill the hole. After a few minutes, others in the group reached for the shovels and so it continued with each man shovelling until he was tired and then passing off the task to another who waited, talking quietly of weather and snow melt and the winter just passed, until it was his turn. The women chatted and watched their children playing around the yard.

It takes a lot of shovelling to fill a grave dug by a backhoe. It was more than half an hour before the dirt neared the top. Turns with the shovel got shorter but more frequent. The mood lightened with the labour. Gradually, most of the women and kids picked up salads and cakes from their cars and joined the folks eating and talking in the house.

Near the end, Frank paused for breath. Leaning on his shovel, he nodded towards the hill behind the house. "Hugh wanted to be buried up there," he said. The sweating men looked up at the knoll where just-budded aspens rustled as they caught a stray breeze from the coast.

"He probably wanted to be able to look down and watch his boys working," drawled another man, and turning, he bent his back to the last shovelful.

Leslie Yates

Leslie Yates has lived over 14 years in Prince Rupert where he is the publisher of *The Prince Rupert Daily News*. A former journalist, his work has covered a wide range of media. "Grounding Time" was inspired by flying experiences on the North Coast.

"Prince Rupert Radio, this is helicopter Fox-Whiskey-Hotel-Yankee."

"Fox-Whiskey-Hotel-Yankee, Prince Rupert Radio. "Go ahead."

"Rupert Radio. Hotel-Yankee is lifting off Seal Cove for a medevac on Gribbell Island. I'd like to file a flight note."

"Hotel-Yankee — winds at the airport are two zero — twenty gusting twenty-five. Barometer is niner decimal three three. Reported traffic is a Beaver over Hunts Inlet for the Cove. Standby for flight note."

"Roger."

"Hotel-Yankee, Prince Rupert Radio, go ahead with note."

"Yes, Rupert Radio. Hotel-Yankee is a Bell 204, details on file at Prince Rupert. Fuel on board two decimal five hours. Itinerary is Gribbell Island via Grenville Channel, half hour on site and return Prince Rupert Hospital via Grenville. SAR action three hours. Time off Seal Cove eighteen zero five. One soul on board, pilot's licence VRD 186003. I'll close the note via VHF at Rupert."

"Ah, Roger Hotel-Yankee, what is your anticipated flight time?"

"Rupert Radio, Hotel-Yankee, two hours ten minutes."

"Roger, Hotel-Yankee. The note's on file."

"Rupert Radio. Hotel-Yankee, when is grounding time?"

"Hotel-Yankee, last light is twenty thirty."

—1—

"Helicopter Hotel-Yankee, this is Beaver Sierra-Alpha. Do you read?"

"This is Hotel-Yankee. Got you loud and clear, Sandy. What's happening?"

"Yeah. Ryan, would you believe I'm approaching Mach One? Over Holland Rock and gallopin' for the barn on a southeast breeze. What're you up to on this foul evening, with the Clydesdale no less?"

"Yeah, Sandy, the details as yet are sketchy. Some guy apparently rode his logging truck over the side and he's in tough shape. They said to bring a long line and all the lifting power we have. So here I am and Joanne's at home steaming. We were just on the way out for dinner."

"One of the joys of the business. How's about me consoling Joanne by the campfire till you get back?"

"Thanks a lot, creep."

"What are friends for? Say, Ryan, I just came from Kitkatla and the weather's the pits. That front they've been waiting for is on the move. Glad I wasn't going farther south."

"Talking to you has been right cheery. See ya later, cowboy."

Click.

—2—

"Gribbell Island, this is Helicopter Hotel-Yankee . . . Davidson Camp? Do you read?"

—3—

"Gribbell Island, this is Helicopter Hotel-Yankee. . . ."

"Hotel-Yankee, this is Davidson Camp on Gribbell Island. Where the hell have you been?"

"Ah, Davidson Camp, who'm I talking to?"

"Stu, the foreman."

"Listen, Stu, I stood my date up to buck this goddam thirty-knot head wind that's been rattling my eyeballs all the way down here. I'm at 400 feet below most of the cloud and can barely see both sides of the channel through the rain. If we're gonna get along on the phone, Stu, you gotta ease up on your openers. My name's Ryan."

"Yeah, yeah. I guess we're all feelin' the strain. That's a friend of mine down over the side. How far out are you?"

"I dunno — five, ten minutes. You'll probably hear me before I see the camp. Let me know if I'm going by."

"Ryan, here's the plan. We got a man pinned under an overturned truck down over a cliff. To make matters worse the truck's landed in a stand of trees that's gonna make it impossible for you to get too close. We gotta get you to lift one end of the truck and then lift him out on a stretcher."

"Okay, Stu. I'll need to set this thing down somewhere. I've got to hook up the long line and jump into the left seat. Will 200 feet be enough?"

"Yeah. Yeah, I hear you now. You must be real close. Do you see the trailer lights? You can land here."

"I've got the camp."

"I hope 200 feet will be enough. He's located a half mile north up the road that follows the shore. I'll leave now. You'll see my pick-up where he's gone over. "

"Right — Oh. Stu — the head wind has made my fuel situation for the return trip touch and go. How bad is this guy?"

"Last I heard he was still alive. There's a couple of guys there with him. He needs to be in a hospital real bad."

"I don't suppose you guys got any Jet B lying around?"

"This ain't exactly Mirabel airport."

—4—

"This is Hotel-Yankee. You there, Stu?"

"Ya. I can hear you, Ryan. We're down over the side."

"I see the pick-up but I don't see anybody."

"Come over the road. We'll turn on a couple of flashlights."

"Jesus, you weren't kidding about the trees. Put the lights where you want the hook. How about doing something about the rain?"

"The line's gotta come down between the trees, Ryan. We're gonna hook you up to the front end of the cab and hope you'll take enough weight off this guy's legs for us to pull him out."

"This thing will only lift four thousand pounds."

"We'll need it all. My men have cut some prys and blocks."

"Comin' down. It's so dark down there. I can't get a good fix on the hook. Whoa, there, girl."

"What was that?"

"Just talking this chariot into keeping her shoulder into the wind. How far is the hook from the truck?"

"You're on the wrong side of these two trees. Bad angle to lift from."

"Okay."

"You've got it now, another 15 or 20 feet."

"Dammit, the skids are practically touching the tree tops."

"Another 10 feet; we'll lengthen our cable."

"That's it, Stu. I'm eyeball to eyeball with the top of this spruce."

"A couple more inches — get up on the engine hood with the sling! Good — okay, Ryan, you're hooked. Wait till my man gets off. There. Okay. Give it hell."

"Here we go — I'm not getting any farther from this tree."

"We still can't get the blocks under."

"I'm pullin' 100 per cent and she isn't likin' it. I'm 500 pounds over limit What's happening?"

"You gotta do better, Ryan, the truck's shifted but we can't free him. Goddamit, don't drop it back down; you'll kill him."

"Alright, alright. I'm pullin'. She's over-torqued and the temperature's climbing. I can't keep it up."

''It's comin', Ryan — jerk it back."

"If something pops there'll be two to pick off the mountain side. We're burning fuel like crazy."

We've got him! The blocks went in — HEY — you two! Get him in the basket — careful with him — watch the ropes don't tangle — strap him tight — Ryan, give us as much slack as you can and we'll hook up the stretcher."

"Comin' down . . . Stu, will ya close your mike button when you're yelling at the boys. You're blowing my ear drums."

"The basket's hooked ''

"Get ready to catch him in case he snags up on one of those trees."

"Easy does it. Wait. Let the basket turn. You'll clear the branch."

"I see it."

"Up. Up. Steady. It's going. You made it."

"I'll set him down at the camp, and a couple of your people can slide him into the back. I won't shut her down."

"How's the fuel?"

"Marginal. The tail wind will help. When you get back to camp, call Rick, the base manager, on the radio-telephone and have him stand-by with the 206 and a drum of fuel. I'll call him on the way back."

"Done."

"You wanna ride back with me?"

"Try me when the weather's better."

—5—

"Rupert Radio, this is Hotel-Yankee."

"Go ahead, Hotel-Yankee."

"Rupert Radio, Hotel-Yankee's over the Lawyer Island Light for the hospital."

"Hotel-Yankee, no reported traffic. Barometer, niner decimal one two. Winds one two zero at thirty gusting to thirty-eight."

"Roger."

"How's the passenger?"

"He's conscious."

"I'll notify the hospital."

—6—

"Rick, Hotel-Yankee, do you read?"

"Yeah, Ryan. Where are you?"

"Comin' up on the Kinahans. If the wind doesn't quit, I'll make the hospital. You better drive that drum of fuel over to the pad. Better refuelling there than on the beach."

"You won't need it tonight — tie the 204 down there."

"What?"

"Grounding time was fifteen minutes ago."

"Damn. Think anyone will complain? It couldn't be helped."

"Did you have a flight note on this one?"

"Yeah."

"Then it's in black and white. You can count on an investigation."

"Just what we need. But I know one fellow that won't be complaining. What about leaving Hotel-Yankee on the pad?"

"I'll talk to them. See you in the morning."

"Will you call Joanne?"

Click.

—7—

"Rupert Radio. Hotel-Yankee is over the hospital. Please close my. . . ."

"Hotel-Yankee, Rupert Radio — how many times do we have to tell you guys to close these flight notes just before landing?"

"But — "

"Hotel-Yankee, we estimated you down twenty-twenty-nine and closed the note."

''Roger, Rupert Radio — and, thanks."

Jean Rysstad

Long-time Prince Rupert resident Jean Rysstad's fiction has been published in a variety of literary magazines and anthologies including *The Journey*, *Prize*, and *Coming Attractions*. Her written works include a collection of short stories, *Travelling In* (Oolichan Books), several series for *Morningside Drama*, CBC Radio, and a stage monologue for the Vancouver View Festival.

"Lovebites" was inspired by the comment, "If you ever do that again, I'll kill you."

Paul and his father are coming in from a ten-day trolling trip. It has been a long ten days without much fish. Five or six in a seventeen-hour day. These northern summer days stretch from five in the morning until near midnight. "Scratching" is what they call this kind of trip once they are in town. That's how Paul's dad will sum it up on the dock to anyone who asks. Paul hasn't had to use the term "scratching" yet this season because until now they've done well. He'd like to be able to be as casual about a bad trip as his dad, but he thinks he'd feel pretty phony, that it would sound fake coming from his mouth — as if he can accept this kind of a trip, that it rolls off him like water.

For Paul, it has been one of the worst trips he can remember. He longs to be home just to have a bath, use the telephone, lay on his own bed instead of a bunk.

The thing is, Paul's dad wants the fish, no matter how many or how few, handled with care. He wants them babied. His dad wants the fish to look and feel like they are still alive and it requires a dedication which Paul doesn't feel this year although he wants the money from the fish more than he has ever wanted it, and he wants more money than he has ever wanted. Though Paul is satisfied that he's done his job, gone through the motions, sharpened and baited, cleaned and iced the same way he always has, he's disappointed both in the trip and in himself.

He has always thought he had what it took to fish but now, half way home, coming across from the Charlottes, he feels like he'll go crazy if something doesn't happen to make the trip go faster. He'd like to be able to say, well, at least this or this happened. But he doesn't know what it could possibly be. The wind is light, the sea is calm, and the weather voice promises more of the same.

Paul shrugs. He guesses he can make it home in one piece, body and soul intact. He guesses he'll live. He'll make it through not just this trip, but the next and the next and the next until the season's over. It gets harder and harder to have a decent trip — or so he's heard until he can't stand it anymore.

His dad could retire, but he keeps on fishing. Paul thinks that his dad expects or hopes that Paul will take the boat when he's through school and Paul thinks or hopes that too. But for the last few days, when it was obvious they weren't going to get much, Paul's been thinking his dad would be better off alone than with him around. He wouldn't have to pay out a share to Paul.

At the galley table below deck, Paul considers the V-shaped birds in flight design he'd drawn on the note pad they keep handy there for grub lists, for marking down gear or lures they want to pick up in town. He's been using a pencil on a string tied through the hole in the shelf above the table. He drilled the hole one trip when the only pencil he could ever find rested on his dad's ear.

On this trip, not even the weather has been anything to speak of. Usually there is a day or two where they have to battle with the weather and Paul doesn't mind this. Then at night, dropping anchor, holing up, is a small celebration. Paul makes hot chocolate. He reads. The bells jangle on the stabilizer poles. The wind is a low-pitched humming song on the rigging.

Paul reads *Popular Mechanics, Consumer's Market* and *Omni*. He likes to compare brand names and performance data of the various items he considers buying with his crew share. He's spent much of his time this summer daydreaming about what he'll be capable of buying. He'll be able to get his driver's licence soon and a car is number one on his want-and-need list. On the last trip, Paul had been comparing Hyundais, Toyotas, small Fords and Chevs. Opening and closing the two-versus-four-door vehicles in his imagination. Definitely two-door, he'd decided. Classier. One for himself and one for a girl whose name he wasn't sure of. It wouldn't be Trish or Kim. He wasn't comfortable with girls who had names like that and most of them did. Cathy or Janey was better. He had a composite picture of this girl drawn from the fifteen or so girls in his grade ten class — taking this item of clothing from one and this way of standing from another. It was a kind of composure of body and mind that he dreamt about in a girl. Or in himself, Paul thinks. He swats the pencil on the string so that it swings wildly back and forth.

Paul goes up to the cabin. His father, at the wheel, greets him, lifts his cap with one hand and runs his fingers through his hair with the other, then sets his cap back on. Paul catches himself about to repeat the same gesture but forces himself to stop mid-way. He doesn't want to be exactly like his father, a copy of his dad, only forty years younger. This kind of calm acceptance of everything, going steady in one direction until it's time to go in another. Paul wishes his dad would do something erratic, surprise him, shock him, but he never does and never will. Without thinking, Paul completes the gesture he consciously stopped himself from making. He realizes what he's done only when he's re-adjusting the peak of his hat to sit firm and tight on his head again.

"Shit," Paul mumbles. It is hopeless for him to try to get back into the dream state for the travelling-in. The dream girl, who last trip wore a blue flowered skirt, those ones with a shy bit of ruffle at the hem, had vanished. The possibility of her was gone. Oh yeah, he remembers, scornfully, she was going to be the kind of girl who found everything interesting. Who never used the words "boring" or "bored." She was the kind of girl who'd like trolling, who could laugh at herself and amuse herself, and not need to be talking all the time.

It was only five days ago that Paul had decided that he should check the daily newspapers, the *Buy and Sells* and the used-car lots to see what was around for cheap. Say $500 to $1000. He considered this a mature, a realistic, assessment of his financial situation. He figured he and his friend Trent could work on this car in mechanics shop at school and at home in the garage.

"I'll take a wheel turn," Paul offers. His dad doesn't hear him. Paul stands closer. "Do you want me to take it for a while?" Paul asks again.

"No," his father says, "But you could put the coffee on."

Paul doesn't like drinking boat coffee or making it. Cold water and a handful of grounds in a saucepan. They use the propane two-burner for coffee, not the oil stove below. Paul watches that the brew doesn't boil for more than a second, then pulls the pan off, adds a touch of cold water, and the grounds settle.

"About three," his father says, meaning his estimate of when they'll get into town. 3 p.m.

Three more hours is what it means to Paul.

"Do you want something to eat?" Paul asks, hoping his dad will say yes. It will give him something to do.

"One of those biscuits would be fine," Paul's father says. "That'll do. We'll let your mother know we're coming in a bit."

The digestive cookies that Paul's father likes are in the cupboard above the burner. Paul passes the box to his dad who fumbles in the corrugated envelope and comes out with the last three. "That's the end of that one," he says with a grin. "Want one?" Paul hates digestives, but he'd like one now. His father knows how to ration, but Paul's eaten all his treats early this trip.

Paul twists the rectangular bag into a figure eight and shoves it into the garbage can. "You're sure you don't want me to do a stretch?" he asks. His father shakes his head and slurps a mouthful of coffee. It seems to Paul that his father knows how much he'd like to take the boat. His father tests him in little ways all the time.

"Okay," Paul shrugs. "I guess I'll try and dig up something to eat. "

All the envelopes of hot chocolate are gone now. There is a can of strawberry milkshake powder in the back corner of the cupboard, but Paul gags when he looks at it. The milk, on ice in the hold, is past date. Paul hates that chalky past-date taste.

His mother will likely put a roast in the oven when she gets their call and he wants pizza. Or maybe Chinese. He closes his eyes and sees the take-out menu. Combos One, Two and Three. NO SUBSTITUTIONS in bold print. He knows he shouldn't test his sanity like this. He's going crazy, climbing walls. Three more hours of himself.

He sits in the cabin doorway, where his back gets the wind. Faces his father's back and he begins a motion. A pushing and rocking forward, pretending his pushing will help them move faster. His father seems to feel this urging behind him because he glances over his shoulder at Paul. "Won't be long," he says. "We're making good time."

Paul stands. He doesn't know why he wants to be in town so badly. It's not like he'll have any time for himself. They have a lot to do and they will be back out within two days if the weather co-operates.

He takes a leak over the side of the boat, surveying first the sky and then the arc of his water. It used to be more fun.

He zips and turns and looks at the cabin, the roof, and remembers when he used to sit up there on nice days, feeling like the luckiest kid in the world. What the hell, he'd climb up there now.

He sits yoga style, then lays down, watches the grey sky and the grey water from this vantage point. He remembers how high it used to seem, how dangerous, when he sat up there as a kid. How awed he used to be by the depth and width of the ocean. In bad weather he used to be afraid but his father never tried to help him over or through a fear. Or maybe he did, by just letting him work it through for himself.

Paul hears his father call his name. He could reach down and knock on the bow window but he doesn't. He doesn't answer the next, sharper call either.

Paul is not sure why he isn't answering immediately and one part of him, the part that is in this world, not lost, overboard, cannot believe his own silence, his refusal to answer his father's calls. He cannot believe himself when he doesn't scramble down and say, "Hey dad, I'm here," when he sees his father stand helpless for a moment at the stern, then hurry to the bow, searching off the side of the boat as he runs.

The boat swings round and Paul has to grab the lines that hold the small dinghy on top of the cabin to keep himself from falling off. He does not think of how ironic it would be if he fell over then, when his father turned the boat. Later, it occurs to him.

He climbs down quietly. Stealthily. He knows it is too late to reverse his disappearance though he hasn't been 'missing' for more than ten minutes. Maybe less. His father would be thinking ten minutes was both a long and short time too. Would be scanning port and starboard with binoculars, first with his glasses on, then off.

Paul speaks loudly from just inside the cabin. "Dad," he says, "It's okay." He walks towards his father because that's where his feet take him. When he comes within arm's length of his dad, he shrugs. He doesn't want his body to shrug. It shocks him.

Into his father's eyes comes first a glossy black welcome, hot tar, thick as blood, which Paul wants to return, which Paul wants to reach for. . . . If only eyes were arms.

But his father's eyes empty at the shrug.

The colour cools, flattens.

His father takes the boat out of gear. He grabs Paul's shoulders, bony under the red and black flannel workshirt and faded black tee-shirt he wears, and shakes.

He shakes Paul by the shoulders and speaks. Staccato:

"If. You. Ever." Jolting the boy with every word, "Do. That. Again." Bones, teeth and brains. "I'll. Kill. You."

Paul's father's hands drop and he turns away from Paul, lifts his cap, puts the boat in gear, ten-knot running speed. He takes a mouthful of the cold grainy coffee Paul'd made for him and spits it out the window.

Paul backs away, trying his shoulders. First one, then the other, in the small warm-up circles he uses before a workout or a run. He lays below deck on the bunk, eyes closed, ears tuned to the drone of the engine. He falls asleep.

When they nuzzle up to the plant dock — as always the perfect, gentle landing — Paul wakes. He thinks he might tell his father that he'll sleep on the boat. That he'll unload, clean up the boat, get ice. He could ask his dad to let him. That way his dad could have a rest, forget about the boat for a day or so and he could try and make it up. He doesn't have the nerve to say anything. He does his usual share. Hoses down the deck and scrubs the checkers, gathers the dirty clothes and the garbage. His mother's waiting above the dock in the pickup. He steps off, knowing he'll have to take his place, seated between them. He walks like he is still on the boat, his sense of balance in transition.

After his father and mother go to bed, Paul runs the bath water. He brings the small television in from the kitchen and sets it on the shelf above the taps, pushing all the varieties of shampoos and rinses and little pink and blue seashell soaps to one side. He hopes the T.V. won't fall in the tub. Then again, it might be good if he got zapped, he thinks. The water pours down hot and clean on his big, stinking feet. He dumps a half bottle of his mother's bath foam under the waterfalls, scoops the foam and blows it. Turns the channel around once and stays with the late night show host, Letterman. The band leader named Paul is the butt of Letterman's jokes, which is fine with the Paul in the tub. He deserves it. There's an Irish actress whose talk is off the wall. The things she says seem to come out of nowhere, from nothing said before or nothing Letterman's asked her. Paul scrubs himself everywhere and gets out of the tub.

He examines his back and shoulders in the three-way hinged mirror above the sink. Eight purple-black-and-blue imprints blossoming like buds. Lovebites. Paul snorts. A subject for Letterman if ever there was one.

He rubs himself with the towel which he hoped would be soft, fluffy, but it isn't. Dried on the line, as usual. His mother still thought towels and sheets dried outside smelled so fresh.

Paul dries every toe, every crack of himself. He's begun to feel better but what is Letterman doing now? Crushing a tube of toothpaste under a ton of weight. The paste spurts out from all the seams. And now a doll. A child volunteers her doll for the 'experiment' and she stands puzzled, frowning as deeply as an old woman.

There is a knock at the bathroom door. Gentle. Paul snaps the T.V. off.

"What?" he says. It was his mother's knock. "What?"

Her slippers shuffle. "I just have to tell you this."

There is a pause between them. "What?" says Paul.

"Once, when I was old enough to know better, I pulled a chair out from beneath my grandmother."

"And what?"

"She fell hard, Paul. She broke her tailbone."

Silence. "Paul?" she asks.

"Okay," Paul says. "Okay. Good night. Good night, Mom."

Nancy Robertson

Writer and photgrapher Nancy Robertson lives in Prince Rupert for half the year and travels south in winter. Her work has appeared in a variety of publications including *Prairie Fire, Room of One's Own, Camera Canada,* and *Photo Life.* Her photography has won several awards; one of her photos graces the cover of this book.

"Indelible" was written following her daughter's return to university after Christmas holidays the first year they were separated.

> We walk the beach
> hand in hand
> The Hunter watches over us
> constant surf
> never ending beach
> involve us
> a part so small
> like grains of sand
> so many
> you couldn't count
> one handful
>
> We turn
> look back
> into the black night
> no trace of our presence
> forgiven
> forgotten
> only the surf's
> final crash
> before spending itself
> along the long beach
> reaching

winding
our footprints
gone forever

Nothing but
sand, sea, and stars
and the memory
of your hand
in mine.

JoAnne Ames

JoAnne Ames was born in Pincher Creek, Alberta, and raised in northwestern B.C. She lives on the Queen Charlotte Islands.

the preface is: this is not a love poem

but i ask myself   why i
rise to the surface of the day
with your eyes in mind,   turn
still asleep
and seek   the shelter of you
warm   the scent & muscle & blood of you
your heart   beat, rhythm of your breath
heat of the first morning kiss
a dream of you   moving over   lying over   me

preface aside: i am awake   hungry
        a black bowl of wanting
only you can fill.

Dorothy Trail Spiller

Dorothy Trail Spiller's first poem was published in *The Vancouver Province* when she was seven years old. Since she retired from the Department of Indian Affairs and moved to the Queen Charlotte Islands, she has been writing full time, at her word processor, looking across dunes and ocean to the mountains of Alaska. Her stories and poems have been published in a number of literary magazines. A novel is now at a publisher's, under consideration.

"We meet so many people in our lives, and we don't really know each other." This is a dramatization of an actual experience.

All of February the wind blew down the Nass River, meeting the waves rolling up from Dixon Entrance, slicing off the crests in white foam so that no float plane could get in to the Reserve.

On the first fine morning in March, I hopped on the Beaver that flies in and out of the village twice a day when weather and tides permit, flew across the mountains to the Nass and up to Git-se-ap.

I needed to discuss the recent Departmental budget cuts with the Chief and Band staff, and had phoned ahead by radio phone to let them know I was coming.

On the boardwalk that leads to the village, I met Gus Allen who, besides being a fisherman, runs the little village-version supermarket. He was on his way to the plane to see if some stock he'd ordered had arrived.

"I hear Sadie's home. How is she?" His wife had recently had a major operation and come home to the Reserve only the week before.

"Pretty good. Linda's looking after the store for her. The boys got their own boats this year."

"How's Daphne?"

"Good. Real good. Finishes grade twelve this year and talking about going to university. The new guy says she's a natural-born teacher."

Gus looked self-conscious. He was very proud of his youngest daughter.

I have nothing to do with the school. It's administered by the local Indian school district, but I'd heard about the previous teacher who'd resigned before Christmas after making some derogatory remarks about his students' ancestors. Apart from any other problems he had, he must have been kind of dumb. At any rate, they'd managed to find someone to take his place and finish out the term. I couldn't help wondering why this new teacher happened to be free halfway through the school year.

"He's a real smart man." Gus nodded to one of the village fishermen on his way down to the floats, loaded with gear, and stood aside to let him pass. "Real good at languages. Already picked up some Nishga and made a speech when we had our banquet after the basketball tournament. Guess you heard we won, eh?"

"I sure did, Gus."

"First time for us. Them guys from Alaska was hard to beat. Steve talked some to the elders in Nishga. Just a few words you know, but pretty good. He talks French and Spanish too, he says, and some other language I never heard of. He can even talk Russki."

"Sounds like a clever man. What's his name?"

"Steve Hakopian. Or something like that."

I knew him. Or had known him. I was immediately back in grade eleven, Spanish One, Steven's clear eyes looking into mine, talking and listening as if we had something worthwhile and important to say to each other.

And Herbert Cooper.

Mr. Herbert Cooper was the teacher. 'Herbie Hots,' the boys called him, although at the time I didn't know why.

He was fat and pale, dressed in a suit of chewing gum grey with wide, flapping trousers, sparse grey hair and large pale ears with a frosty look to them, fingers like fat, white worms crawling across the paper, rubber soled shoes creeping up and down the aisles. But you always knew he was there, behind you, when his breath wafted across your shoulder.

This was a time, you understand, when everyone was — I was going to say 'more innocent' — but perhaps 'ignorant' would be truer. I was young for my age and in many ways more ignorant than the norm, even then. But I was good at languages. I loved words. Any words in any language. And Spanish was so easy.

What I liked about it was the way it obeyed all its own rules but alas, easy come, easy go. Now all I can remember are two proverbs, 'No se aventura, no pasa la mar,' loosely translated as 'Nothing ventured, nothing gained,' and 'En boca cerrada, no entran moscas,' ('In a closed mouth, no flies enter.')

Because I was confident that I knew how to manage words, I welcomed Mr. Cooper's presence at my side reading my first attempt at Spanish composition, even though his breath was distracting so that I had to turn my head away.

His fat fingers pointed out an error and as they withdrew, brushed across my chest.

I shivered and slid over to the far side of my seat. An accident, I thought, but I was disturbed by the queer feelings aroused in me. Revulsion. Nausea. And something else.

It happened again. And again. Casually, almost unnoticeable. Except by me. Surely it couldn't always be accidental? But he hadn't really done anything. I thought I must be imagining it and wondered why I had such awful, depraved thoughts. Mr. Cooper was supposed to be a good teacher.

One day when he passed my desk, his hand secretly cupped my breast and squeezed. I could no longer pretend it was an accident.

I knew I should do something, but I wasn't sure what. I wanted to tell my parents, but my father was a hot-tempered man. He would explode with rage and come storming up to the school. Everyone would know! I would be branded, pointed out, talked about. So I said nothing, just hoping the whole problem would go away.

A few days later, at the end of Spanish period, everyone was hurrying to change classes. I was gathering up my papers and stopped to check my timetable. Study period next. I was almost the last one out, and as I headed for the hall, I had to pass Mr. Cooper who stood in the doorway. As I brushed past him, he took my arm.

"Your composition needs some work," he said. "Come after last period and I'll go over it with you."

There was no mistake this time about where those fingers were searching.

"Stop," I hissed, and pulled away.

Clutching my books, I rushed down the hall to the girls' washroom, and dumped my books on the ledge between two wash basins. I turned on the tap, splashing cold water on my hands and face, trying to wash away the burning shame. I spent the whole of the study period in the washroom.

Mr. Cooper gave me no more trouble. He was probably frightened by what he had done.

Shortly after that, a new boy enrolled in the class. His father was some sort of low-level diplomat from one of the middle-eastern countries. He already spoke Spanish, along with French, Russian, Farsi, and of course, English. He was only enrolling in Spanish to get credits.

He seemed to have nothing in common with the rest of the class. Even his appearance was different. More mature, tall, with broad shoulders and narrow hips, a thatch of gold-brown curls, a narrow, aristocratic nose and beautiful wide-spaced hazel eyes. He was intelligent, educated, worldly in the best sense, and he wrote poetry and stories for fun. His name was Steven Hakopian.

Before class, he would come over to my desk and talk to me about poetry and writing.

"You are a clever girl, Charlotte," he would say. "You must use your ability. Don't waste it. Let it grow. I think one day you will do something wonderful."

I was sustained by his interest, and in its warmth grew relaxed and confident. His conversation finally bridged the gap for me between the strands of lingering childhood and the emotions of an adult. Without ever having to examine them again, the dark, ugly thoughts, the barely understood taint of Mr. Cooper, seemed to have been washed away. I felt clean once more.

I never thought I was 'in love' with Steven. That always went with movies and being asked to school dances, or holding hands in the corridors between classes, but years later I knew this had been a real love.

When Steven said goodbye after the final class that term, I didn't know he wouldn't be coming back.

I used to think that one day he would be a great writer, and I watched for his name in book reviews, but eventually other things happened to me and the memory of that year receded into the background of my life.

So. He had become a teacher and now, in the middle of the term, he had come to teach in a school on an Indian Reserve. I became anxious to see him again. I wanted to tell him how much he had meant to me at that particular time in my life.

The meeting with the Band Council was over by the middle of the afternoon. School was out and the plane wasn't coming for me until four o'clock, so I walked over to the teacherage where Gus had told me Steven was living, and knocked on his door.

He was not as tall as I remembered. His shoulders were slightly stooped and his hair not such a bright, golden brown. In fact, there was a lot of grey in it. But his eyes were the same.

"Yes?" His faint, rather distant smile never reached his eyes.

"I don't suppose you remember me," I began, "but are you the Steven Hakopian who took Spanish at Kerrisdale High in Mr. Cooper's class about thirty-five years ago?"

"Ye-es," he hesitated but made no move to invite me in.

"I'm Charlotte Cox? Used to be Charlotte McKenzie? We used to talk together a lot before class about writing and poetry?"

He still looked uncertain. "Will you come in and have a cup of tea?"

He stood aside and I followed him into the living room, furnished in typically Indian Affairs style left over from the days when the Department took care of everything. There was the beige, brown and orange, chintz-covered Colonial chesterfield, the maple coffee and end tables, the cream shaded lamp, the green scatter rug on the beige linoleum floor, and that was about it.

I sat at one end of the chesterfield and waited in silence while Steven went into the kitchen and made tea. He came out and set a potholder on the coffee table, under the hot teapot. Then he returned to the kitchen for two mugs, a can of milk, and a box of sugar cubes.

When he came back, he swished the pot around a bit then poured the tea, still in silence.

I began to feel awkward and wished I hadn't come, but it was too late to retreat now so I plunged on.

"I guess I remember you because you came in the middle of the term, and you seemed so much more grown up than the rest of us."

There was such a long silence I thought he wasn't going to answer me.

"I moved around a lot," he explained at last. "My father was a clerk at the consulate."

"Yes, I'd heard something like that."

He was quiet again, his beautiful eyes blank as if his thoughts had turned inward. I wondered if he was searching for memories or had merely retreated from an unwanted intrusion.

"My father and mother spent their lives in other people's countries," he said after a while. "I hardly knew my own country. The last time, they went home without me."

"No matter," I assured him with a senseless heartiness that I never normally used. "I just thought I'd drop in to say hello while I'm waiting for the plane to pick me up. I didn't mean to bother you, or keep you from anything."

I had imagined I would tell him about my marriage, my children (now grown), my job, (where I was bogged down at a lower management level with no real hope of ever rising higher). A sort of success, but not the vistas of achievement he had once envisioned for me. Even, I thought, I would confide to him with a smile, about my feelings towards the boy that he had been, and why it had mattered so much to have known him. But how could I when he didn't remember me? A flush rose to my face at my own memory of Spanish One.

I couldn't bring myself to ask what he'd been doing since we last saw each other. It would have seemed a monstrous invasion. I don't know why this was so, because as a boy he'd been open enough. Of course, he had never told me anything about himself, except that he liked to write. Our talk had always been about feelings and ideas, never about persons and events.

"Would you like some more tea?"

"I used to look for your name on the covers of books," I finally ventured, smiling at him as I held out my mug. "You remember, you wanted to be a writer?"

He shook his head. "I gave that up a long time ago."

I wondered if he was married. There was certainly no woman here. The most indifferent housekeeper would have made some impact on this room which had about as much personality as a dentist's waiting room. I looked around. No books, no music, no pictures. Steven had given nothing to it.

He seemed to have brought nothing of his own from the past, and the thought that I had wanted to blurt out intimate revelations, to a man who had turned into a total stranger, made me feel embarrassed and ashamed once more. I thought all those feelings had been dealt with long ago.

Then I heard the sound of the plane as it buzzed the village before circling over the river and coming in for a landing at the floats.

"There it is," I said, jumping up, happy to have something to say, something to do. "Thanks for the tea."

He came with me to the front steps.

"I'm sorry," he said. "So much happened to me. I remember —" a flicker of what might have been recognition crossed his face, but by then all I wanted to do was get away and not miss my plane.

As I hurried down the path he stood watching me.

By the time I had climbed into the back seat of the Beaver and buckled my seat belt, my embarrassment had dissipated.

He had looked weary, as if he suffered a lot of pain. Well, we all suffered pain at one time or another. Some of us talked about it and some didn't. The affection and gratitude I had felt for him was hidden away as much as the other things.

Next time I go to Git-se-ap, I decided, I'd see Steven again and find out if that flicker of recognition had been real.

However, summer came and went, and one day during the noon hour in early fall, I met Gus and Sadie on Third Avenue. They'd come into Prince Rupert to do some shopping and we stood talking.

Sadie was well and seemed to have completely recovered from her operation. Linda was married now, and both the boys had had a good fishing season. Daphne was enrolled at UBC in the education program.

"I'm so glad," I said. "That teacher, Steven Hakopian, must have been a good influence. Is he back in the school this year?"

"No," explained Gus. "We were sort of sorry to see him go, but he was only filling in. We had a couple of our own people ready to teach. Got their Bachelor of Education and everything. One of them applied for Steve's job."

"That's great," I said.

Twice, Steve had bumped against my life and drifted away again. They used to call them D. P.'s after the war. Displaced persons. I suppose that's what Steven Hakopian must have been. Even after all these years. Unsettled. Dislocated. Displaced.

Kenneth Campbell

I chose a stone
Mute cold
Wide as the butt of a cedar tree
At the edge of the shore,
Moving between two worlds
On the tide

I picked and chipped,
A face
Emerged
Stared out from hollow eyes
Flecked with mica tears

I formed a granite fin
Stone-spirit trembled and shook
I leaped on its back
Grasping the fin
Dove with it beneath the sea

And beneath the tide
Shimmering lairs of
Hiding unknown forms
Iridescent eyes peered out of
Green-spun universes
Then rushed me back to the biting air

I released the fin
Stone-spirit trembled and shook
The granite cracked
An impatient mouth
Swallowed me up
And now I stare through hollow eyes
I am a stone
At the edge of the shore
Moving between two worlds
On the tide

Dorothy Trail Spiller

A deserted river beach and the Easter Sunday tradition of Native villagers walking through their village streets singing inspired this story.

Eva Tommy comes home for the funeral. After the other sons and daughters, brothers and sisters, uncles and aunts have left, Eva stays behind to find someone to look after her son, but no one in the village has room for him.

Johnny is five years old. He doesn't know his mother very well, because he's lived all his life with his great grandmother, Selena Tommy.

"Can't I live with you?" he asks, but his mother shakes her head. Her new man won't let her have any kids stay with them. Finally, an aunty who lives at the cannery all year round sends word that she'll take him.

His mother puts a message out on the radio, and the man comes to fetch them back to the cannery. At least Johnny will be living near his mother now, and can see her sometimes.

The Reserve where he's lived all his life is an isolated one, bounded by the river, the mountains, and the forest, accessible only by small fish boats, sea planes, and helicopters.

His mother's own mother died when she was a baby. When his mother was sixteen, she went to work in a cannery and has stayed there, or in the nearby city, ever since. She came home once, just before her little boy was born, but left Johnny to Selena, her grandmother, to bring up.

The farthest he's ever been from home before is to the mouth of their river in the spring, when the oolichan are running. He'd loved the excitement of the half wild camp, the fish as they hurtled towards the shore in shining thousands to spawn and die, the pungent smell of the rotting flesh being rendered into grease in cooking vats over the fires, the hysterical, swooping, screeching gulls.

That was the only time Grandmother would leave the village, but she took him everywhere she did go, berry picking, collecting bark and roots, digging for clams, and plucking mussels from the rocks. Every Sunday she dressed him in his best green sweater that she had knitted for him herself, and took him with her to church. That was especially wonderful at Christmas. But Easter was nice too.

On Easter Sunday, as the sun rose, the villagers walked through the streets singing, "My Lord is Risen." The little boy, full of mysterious happiness, walked with them, clinging to Grandmother's twisted old fingers, shivering a little in the morning wind from the river.

In summer, the men from the village always went away to fish, and most of the women went to the canneries to work, taking the children with them, but Grandmother always refused to leave the Reserve. Johnny couldn't help feeling a little lonely then.

Grandmother didn't like the city, or the cannery towns, or the big river to the south of their own. There was nothing in the white man's stores she couldn't get from the catalogue, she told Johnny, and she was afraid of the drinking that went on during the fishing season.

Johnny always wondered if 'out there' was anything like the movie pictures that they showed Friday nights at the Community Hall. He begged Grandmother to go with the others so he could see the cars and the trains, the buildings, and the coloured lights. He listened a little enviously when the other children came back in the fall, to go to the village school, and talked about the place where you could go and sit, and order anything you wanted to eat: ice cream, hamburgers, anything. And the stores! Where they had whole counters full of different kinds of chocolate bars, not just one or two boxes like the village store.

Now, Johnny thinks, he will see all this for himself, but he doesn't feel as happy and excited about it as he might have, because this Easter they went out as usual, singing through the village, and Grandmother caught a cold. She refused to be flown out to the hospital, and died. Still, Johnny is proud to step onto the man's boat and wave goodbye to the village, because at last he's going to see what the rest of the world is like.

He thinks how pretty his mother looks as she hands over his two boxes, one for his clothes, one for his toys, to stow below the deck. She's wearing a bright red coat that her new man has bought for her. Her black hair, caught in a knot on top of her head and hanging down her back, lifts gently in the river wind, and strands blow about her round, smooth cheeks.

Johnny has an almost new jean jacket himself, but he's been growing so fast the sleeves are too short.

It's a long trip to the big river and the cannery. Down their own river, down the narrow inlet, into the Sound. They pass other villages on other Reserves, some of them much bigger than their own. The open water rolling in from the Straits tosses the little boat up and down, and Johnny scrambles excitedly to the railing to watch the great, green waves sliding under the keel.

"Be careful," warns his mother. "Don't fall in."

"Put him below," orders the man. "He's in the way on deck."

Johnny doesn't want to go, but the man is so mean looking. He's not a very nice man. He has skimpy, yellow hair, a bony, red face, and angry blue eyes; and he's been drinking all day from a jug of red wine.

Johnny isn't afraid of the wind and the water, but he doesn't like being in the narrow fo'c's'le, crowded with bunks, sink, oil stove, and the big, dirty, pounding engine. He keeps asking if he can come on deck now, and the man gets even madder than he was before.

Johnny can hear his mother and the man up in the wheelhouse arguing. Before going up river to the cannery, she wants to gather fish eggs to take to her sister. The man wants to go straight to the cannery, so they will have time to catch the bus back to town before the beer parlours close.

The man finally agrees to let her have her way if she will put Johnny ashore to play while they go back to the city liquor store for another jug. Johnny really begins to cry now.

"I'm sure as hell not goin' to listen to that shit no more," says the man angrily. "Put him ashore. There's a beach over there. He can play on that till we get back."

He spins the wheel to avoid a deadhead. "I can't stand candy-ass kids. It'd drive me nuts to listen to him all the way to town and back. If you want fish eggs, we got to go back for a jug. Make up your mind. What's it going to be?"

Eva looks at the beach, hesitating, raising her hand to brush her hair back from her face. She calls Johnny on deck.

"That's a nice beach," she tells him. "Would you like to play there? We'll come back for you as soon as we get the fish eggs for your aunty."

He tries to pull his hands into the sleeves of his jacket to keep them warm, and looks across the water to the shallow crescent of young trees in early leaf. Then he looks anxiously at his mother.

"We won't be very long," she assures him.

Johnny nods wordlessly and turns his head away.

"All right," his mother tells the man.

The man swings the wheel hard over, and the boat heads for shore.

"You mustn't go away from the beach," Eva warns him. "There's railway tracks behind those bushes, and the cannery road's on the other side of the trees. You mustn't cross the tracks. You hear me? A train might come along and run over you. Do you know what happened to your Uncle Reggie? He fell asleep on the tracks and a train cut off his head. You wouldn't like that, would you? They couldn't even find his head at first. It rolled into a ditch."

Johnny shivers.

"I won't cross the tracks," he promises.

The beach falls sharply away at each end, and the man brings the boat in close. While he holds it from the banks with a pike pole, Johnny climbs over the rail, and his mother gives him her hand to help him ashore.

She waves as the boat swings out again into the stream. He blinks his large, black eyes, determined not to cry. He's been trying not to cry ever since Grandmother died.

The beach is small and ridged with dried mud and wavering green lines. It's quite near the mouth of the river, and the pieces of driftwood left by the tide are twisted into shapes like the animals in Grandmother's stories: a fanged wolf, a leaping salmon, and the crested head of a screaming jay.

At first, when the noise of the boat's engine has gone, it seems very quiet. Johnny stands listening as the wind ruffles his thick, straight, black hair. Then he begins to hear the whisper of the river running past, the rustling of the new leaves, and the cry of ravens.

Another sound, a distant, steady hum, grows nearer and nearer — whoosh — then fades away into the distance. He wonders what it is. In a moment or two it's repeated. Then again, only this time coming from the other direction.

He walks fearfully to the thick screen of bushes, and parts them. He can see the terrible, shining railway tracks stretching in both directions, out of sight. Beyond, is the road. A car goes by. That was what made the hum and whoosh. Johnny has never seen a car before. He has toy cars to play with, and he's seen them in the Friday movies, but this is the first real one he's ever seen.

He lets the bushes spring back into place, hiding the tracks and the road, and returns to the beach. The tide is going out. For a while he digs holes in the sand with a flat piece of stick and watches them fill with muddy water. Then he digs canals connecting the holes. He even tries to build a tunnel, but the walls keep collapsing. This isn't really much fun. He's becoming very dirty and wet and wipes his hands on his best green sweater which is the only dry thing about him. Then he looks around for something else to do.

He peeps through the bushes once more and thinks unwillingly of Uncle Reggie's head, dripping blood, with wild eyes, rolling along the ground beside the tracks. He wonders if it was here that the head fell into the ditch. He draws back shuddering.

There doesn't seem to be anything more to do, so he sits down with his back to the roots of an upended tree to wait for the boat to return. He's hungry. And now that he's sitting still, very cold.

It seems to him that he sits there for hours before he hears the beat of an engine, and he sighs with relief. When the boat comes into sight around the bend in the river, he sees that the net drum is covered with branches frosted the fish eggs, and he smiles happily. Now they can go straight to the cannery. For a moment he can't see anyone on deck. He stands up anxiously and runs to the water's edge, so that he'll be ready and not keep the man waiting.

Then the man comes out of the wheelhouse, carrying an empty wine bottle. He seems to have trouble standing up. He clings to the wheelhouse rail, balanced on the narrow footing, and heaves the jug into the air. It sails in a wide curve over the water, and the man, his head tilted to follow it, slips and clutches at the rail. As the jug hits the water there is an even greater splash. The man falls in.

Eva Tommy rushes out of the wheelhouse as the man bobs to the surface. He reaches up his hands, calling, "You bitch. Look what you done."

She bends to help as he grabs at her hands and pulls her in on top of him. They thrash around for a moment in the swift water and then disappear. The boat, with no one to guide it, swings in a slow circle over the place where they have been sucked under. The boat trembles as it hits a deadhead, straightens, and ploughs back down the river.

Johnny waits fearfully, intently watching the patch of water where it all happened. Then he blinks, and when he looks again, he can't be sure just where his mother and the man disappeared. All that can be seen now is murky water and the tumultuous mountains on the far shore. All that can be heard is the sulky quarrelling of the ravens and the broken hum of cars on the road behind him.

His feet feel wet and he looks down. A moment ago he was standing at the water's edge. Now the water covers the soles of his shoes. The tide is coming in. He finds a little stick and stands it upright in the sand at the lip of the water, then moves back up the beach.

It's getting dark now. He peers through the bushes again and sees the tracks still gleaming in the dusk. Beyond, the headlights of cars swing grandly over the horizon. He shivers and wonders what to do.

He wants to tell someone. If only the tracks weren't there, he could go out to the road and wave at a car. Maybe someone would stop, although there is such a tight feeling in his throat, he's not sure he can talk. But he has to tell someone.

He wants Grandmother. He wants to feel her rough, dry hand and see her soft little smile. He wants to bury his face in the black-skirted lap and cry.

Because she was one of the very few old people who never learned to speak English comfortably, she always talked to her grandson in the soft, sibilant tongue of the Tsimshian, telling him stories about the people from long ago. He boasted to her then about how brave he would have been paddling across the Straits in the big war canoes to fight the warriors from the Islands, and nothing in the sea or on the land could make him afraid.

He doesn't want to be frightened now, but he is. He looks at the water moving darkly under the evening sky. It has crept past the stick. He goes back to the water's edge to move it further up the sand, as if by doing so he can make believe the water isn't really coming any closer. How much higher will it rise? To the tracks? What will he do if the water reaches the tracks? And he has no place to go? Dreadfully afraid.

The darkness of the distant mountains has disappeared into the darkness of the sky so that the river seems to stretch away over the rim of the world, yet every minute creeping closer to him.

The beach is full of terrifying shapes, nameless things from Grandmother's tales. When she talked about them, he knew he was brave and fearless, the way those old people had been, but then he'd been safe in her kitchen, rocked in her lap with her arms about him.

Under the water, who knows what dreadful things lurk? Is the man still there? Just below the surface? And his mother? Are they floating under the water? Is that his mother's long black hair drifting toward the beach? Will they come out of the river, wet and shining, dark, and dripping with weed?

He turns blindly and runs from the water. As he plunges into the bushes, he sees once more the glint of the tracks in the starlight, the shining eyeballs, the dark, sticky blood. He whimpers and looks over his shoulder.

The water crawls up the beach, covering the driftwood, blotting out its shapes.

The moon hasn't risen yet, so the light of the cars whizzing past only make the rest of the world darker and more fearsome. He shudders and begins to make little choking sobs. The night wind from the river strikes through his thin clothes. He is so cold. The bushes sag beneath his body, and he curls up beneath their protection, shivering, whimpering, and hiccuping, listening to the darkness, full of the voices of dead Tsimshian.

Finally, the rhythm of the passing cars overwhelms the monstrousness of his fear, and he falls asleep, cradled on branches of thimbleberry, huckleberry, and young alder.

He sleeps for a long time. The cars going by dwindle and cease. The people have all gone home, and the road will be empty until morning. The river laps up almost to the bushes where Johnny huddles in sleep, then turns and goes back the way it has come, over the wet sand.

The moon rises over the mountains on the far shore so that once more the sky is flooded with light, until it too, fades into the light of morning.

Johnny wakes up. For a moment he can't remember why he is here.

He kneels and looks at the river. There is nothing there except water, mountains, and sky. No long black hair floating on the tide. No terrible skinny man stretching out his skinny white arms.

Behind him, the tracks still stretch shining and empty in either direction. He hears a car coming and parts the bushes to look at it disappearing down the road.

His aunty must wonder where he is. Why he hasn't come to stay with her. He wants to get to her and tell her what happened. He steps through the bushes and puts one foot fearfully down on the track. Nothing happens. He puts the other foot down on the track. Nothing happens. He puts the first foot down on the ties, then bravely scrambles across and jumps to the strip of grass at the edge of the road.

When he reaches his aunty, he'll tell her that his mother and the man were bringing her fish eggs, but they got left on the boat.

Barrie Abbott

Barrie Abbott now lives in Vancouver where he is involved in the TV and movie industry. His latest project is a screenplay.

While working as editor of *Houston Today*, he wrote "Northerners versus Nuppies" which enjoyed popularity across the country.

A couple of months ago, on the people's radio network, some northern media luminaries were speculating about what Smithers residents should be called.

Smithereens was, of course, the natural answer, but something far more interesting came out of that discussion. One of those engaged in the conversation used a term, when referring to Smithereens, that I had never heard before: Nuppie.

Nuppie, as in Northern Urban Professional — a variation of Yuppie, which has become common fare. Yuppie has also spawned Yuffies (Young Urban Failures), Huppies (Homeless Urban Professionals), Huffies (Homeless Urban Failures), and so on. The list is longer than a Yuppie's list of CDs. But Nuppie caught me up short.

Specifically, the panel noted that Smithers, supposedly has the highest number of PhDs per capita in Canada. That may be true, and if it is, that is Smithers' particular cross to bear, but it makes the town an anomaly — a northern town without an overwhelmingly high proportion of blue-collar workers. In other words, Smithers has more Nuppies than Northerners.

In Houston, just 50 kilometres south, where I live, we tend to think Smithers also has one of the north's highest rates of smugness. (It also has enough airborne particulate to match Southern California, but I wouldn't say that in public. Heck, they might pull strings, and arrange things so we can't get any more pesto sauce in Houston. But I digress.)

Follow along with me and I will try to show just what sets Nuppies apart from Northerners.

Clothes: Nuppies always dress stylishly, usually L. L. Bean catalogue style. Northerners tend to dress for utility — Fields and Workwear World. A Nuppie will never wear a team jacket unless it says New York or Los Angeles on it. A Northerner is proud to wear a hometown hockey team jacket.

Male Northerners wear baseball caps emblazoned with a logging company logo or the name of a fishing lodge. If not actually born with a cap molded on to his head, then the male Northerner has one in place long before he gets to school. And it won't come off until he dies, except for the day he gets married, shortly after high school, when it will be off for one day. The only baseball-style cap a Nuppie will wear has to have New York, or yes, Los Angles, written on it.

Northerners wear boots to work and white high-tops for casual, but do not lace up either. Nuppies lace up their shoes and boots. This might have something to do with the fact that Northerners get their feet dirtier than Nuppies, and take their shoes off in the mud porch when they enter a house.

Greetings: An opening conversational gambit in the fall in Houston might be, "Ja get yer moose?" This refers, of course, to the Northerner's love of moose hunting, not to mention the love of a freezerful of moose.

A similar conversational opener in Smithers might be, "I say, did you see the list of films coming to town at the next progressive, smarty-pants film festival?" (By the way, Nuppies watch films, Northerners see movies or shows.)

Transportation: Northerners find it perfectly acceptable, and great fun, spending the weekend skidooing or ATVing. Nuppies tend to disdain motorized transport in the bush — they ski or hike. Same on the water. Nuppies tend to paddle canoes and kayaks, whereas Northerners like motor boats.

You can tell the difference between Nuppies and Northerners by what they drive. A typical Nuppie vehicle is a four-wheel-drive Japanese jeep, while a Northerner drives a four-wheel-drive American truck.

Radio: What are they listening to in their respective four-wheel-drives? Nuppies tune in to CBC, morning, noon and night. Northerners only listen to two kinds of music: country and western.

Fishing: If Nuppies engage in this pastime, it will almost always be of the fly-fishing variety. Northerners don't mind chucking hardware or babying a floating flyline, but if they do fly-fish, it tends not to be treated as a religious experience. Nuppies are catch-and-release types. Northerners like to eat what they catch.

Hunting: Northerners do it, Nuppies don't. Nuppies maybe would, but only if it were conducted in the same way as catch-and-release fishing. That raises the question: How would they do it? Rubber bullets? Tranquilizer darts? Shooting a moose — or anything else — for a Nuppie, always refers to taking pictures.

Parking: Nuppies drive straight in: Northerners tend to back into a parking spot. No one can explain why Northerners do this. Is it a circle-the-wagons mentality? Is it so they can clean a moose after dark?

Chainsaws: Northerners and Nuppies both own chainsaws. Northerners, however, usually own more than one, always have plenty of parts around and are not averse to keeping parts on the kitchen table.

Dogs: A Northerner dog travels in the open back of a pickup truck, sometimes on top of the tool box, surfer style. Most Northerner dogs will perform a quick hand removal if you reach into the truck box.

A Nuppie dog has its own blanket, or a special burlap sack, ordered from an American mail-order house, filled with cedar shavings, in the back of a late-model Japanese four-by-four.

Cats: Both Northerners and Nuppies can have one or more of these animals, but a Northerner's cat tends not to have a name, because a Northerner knows that there is no point in giving a cat a name. Northerners' cats tend not to have ear tips either.

Reconciliation: Some nervous Nellies have expressed fears that class warfare could break out between Nuppies and Northerners. As a result, a move has been launched to bring Northerners and Nuppies closer together in order to foster mutual understanding.

The plan, simplicity itself, will have busloads of Smithereens (Nuppies) bused to Houston to spend an evening at the Legion, where they will drink draft beer and play darts. Busloads of Houstonians (Northerners) will be shipped to Smithers and will spend an afternoon at Java's, a popular coffee house. The Houstonians will drink cappuccinos and listen to the piped-in harp music and fugues so beloved of the Nuppies.

It is hoped that this exchange program will bring harmony to the two groups.

Nancy Robertson

The author's first published story, "Familiar Trails" was inspired by the comment, "You did not think that."

We walk, my son and I. We walk because we want to. We have no destination or any set route. It is snowing. The snow is thick and wet and lands and sticks like mud splashed out of a puddle. Street lights look as if they have streamers drifting out like the Maypole Dance I remember as a kid. The evening is full of people. Always is, first snow. Only snow, maybe. Will it last? Christmas is usually grey. Or sheets of rain.

Our footsteps follow familiar trails. Across the bridge, up the hill, behind Booth School, along Sixth Avenue towards Acropolis Hill. Lights from Roosevelt School at the end of Sixth illuminate the oversized snowflakes both inside and out. The main doors open and young children pour out into the night. Parents follow at a more leisurely pace, discussing the concert, their kids, jobs, recipes, and now the weather. Gasps of astonishment. Some with delight, others with groans. Once outside, the crowd disperses easily. Somehow, the right kids end up with the right parents in the right cars. The families that walk, spread apart quickly, and disappear into the night. Their voices carry a soft tune in the dark. As we round the hill and come towards the viewpoint overlooking the harbour and downtown, we hear the last engines start and see headlights slicing through the snow.

Walking in front of us is a mother and her son. He is young, but not young like the little kids. Older, but still no one listens to him. His pants are always too short and his shoes never fit anymore. He is outgrowing his elementary school the same way.

She is angry. Her voice breaks the evening.

"Why didn't you sing in the choir?"

"I don't know." His feet sulk across the snow packed sidewalk.

"You were supposed to."

"I thought it was stupid."

"You did not think that!" and like slow motion her arm rises, her hand opens, her fingers extend and I feel like all the wind is being knocked out of me.

*　　*　　*

When I was a kid, about the same age, I climbed a gravel pit with two of my brothers. It was huge and steep through my eyes then, although if I went back and looked at it today, I would probably be amazed how small and gently sloped it was. My brothers were already on top and yelling at me to hurry up. I didn't like heights, scared I would fall as I scrambled up the first part, slipping a bit on the loose gravel, but climbing easily still. As the incline increased, my pace slowed and I used my hands to help pull myself up. Almost to the top, I looked down. The ground was like a magnet and I was a piece of steel. I landed flat on my back. Gravel showered down the embankment as my brothers rolled and bumped their way down.

"Are you okay?" they shouted. "Are you okay?"

I couldn't say a word. I couldn't breathe. I could see the fright in their eyes and feel the tears trickle across my ears from mine.

It didn't take long to get my wind back, but I was scared. My brothers packed me home. I was too frightened to talk when Mom asked what happened. But this kind of frightened wasn't the same as the other kind. This was the kind that I thought I would be in trouble. My brothers felt that kind, too. They never wanted me to tag along because if anything happened to me, they knew they would be in trouble. So I didn't talk and they talked too fast. I got put to bed and they got sent to their room.

After a while I wasn't scared anymore and was getting bored. It was a hot summer day and from my upstairs window I could see the leaves vibrating on the branches and the branches waving to the sky. But I didn't want to give up my position of importance at that moment. So I kept on pretending that I couldn't talk and spent the afternoon lying on my bed. Mom came and checked on me from time to time but I kept my eyes closed so she wouldn't see any truth in them.

I heard Mom talking to my brothers, then quietly they all went downstairs. The back screen door slammed so I knew they were forgiven and off again without the drudgery of a little sister to look after.

I wanted to go. But I lay on my bed thinking about what it would be like if I never had to talk again. How it would feel not to have to answer any questions. Especially the ones that I didn't want to answer. Where have you been? Why are you late? Why didn't you do your chores? I must have fallen asleep because the noise of the suppertime household woke me. Dad was home from the office, my older and younger brothers home from summer jobs or play; and the scramble for attention from each other almost made me run down the stairs to join the telling of the day's activities. I wanted to. But I didn't.

Mom came up to ask if I wanted supper. I shook my head. Dad came up, sat on the edge of the bed and asked me how I was. I didn't answer. He stroked the hair off my forehead, then bent and kissed me there before the hair fell back in place. He left, and I savoured the control I felt.

I heard my brother, Rob, holler from the kitchen, "Oh boy! Oh boy! Corn-on-the-cob! Oh boy! Oh boy! Corn-on-the-cob!"

Now corn-on-the-cob was my favourite. I loved corn-on-the-cob. Balancing the scales between corn-on-the-cob and the status I was feeling, the scale tipped toward the corn.

I slowly stepped down the stairs, weakly walked into the dining room and announced very softly that I thought I would be able to eat a little supper.

They laughed. All of them. My younger brothers pointed their fingers at me from their extended arms and covered their mouths with their hands and haw-haw-hawed at me, their fingers and hands shaking to the sound of the haw haws.

"You think we're stu-pid!" they chanted.

"You don't know what I think!" I screamed, and ran back upstairs, knowing that the wind had been knocked out of me.

*　　*　　*

The boy catches the slap on the side of his head. He staggers from the suddenness of the action. Lunges forward as if from a crouch. He turns swiftly and glares at her.

"You don't know what I think!" And he runs away with quick strides around the bend in the road and disappears down the stairs that are the short-cut to downtown.

The woman keeps walking, but I know her eyes glisten in the artificial light as if snowflakes have landed on her eyelashes.

We stop at the lookout and sweep snow from a park bench with our mittened hands. We sit close together and watch the snow falling over the city lights. Every few minutes a car slithers by, its wipers groaning under the unfamiliar weight.

"It makes me mad!" he says, and I wonder if I ever did that to him when he was younger. When I knew I was losing control of him. When I didn't feel comfortable with the decisions he was making.

I reach for his hand and hold it in both of mine. I tell him the story of the gravel pit. "What happened?" he asks.

"Oh, they coaxed me back downstairs. I had supper with them and had a lot of fun poked at me. I got to tell about the gravel pit and my brothers got to tell their version. We all caught hell and were told to stay away from there before someone got seriously hurt. And I got over the other hurt, too."

Warm wind brushes my face. "Let's go," I say, "or we're going to get drenched."

We walk, my son and I, back the way we came. Familiar trails. The wet snow changes to rain. It happens so gradually that I can't tell at what point the transition is made.

Grace Hols

"There are many varieties of twosomes, and all kinds of them can work."

1.

Beth thinks everything should have a point. "What for?" she asks. "What would be the point?"

For example, George likes to walk just because he feels like it. Beth goes along to pick berries. On their way back, George carries the pail for her, although he stood, hands in pockets, listening to the birds while she picked. When they get back, George stretches luxuriously and says, "That was great," but Beth has to deal with what to do with the berries. She doesn't even like berries. (George, however, during winter months, spreads thick layers of the homemade jam on his toast and licks his fingers noisily, remembering the birds.)

They decide, this year, to take their vacation in July. George wants water and sun. Beth wants to come home having accomplished something. It is always like this with them. Their lives parallel, although their interests rarely converge. They go on together, side by side, but separate. Like railroad tracks.

Anyway, George drives, and Beth is no good with maps. They find water on Vancouver Island, and settle back to wait for the sun.

Beth says, "There are tours on the hour every hour," reading to George without looking up from the brochure.

But George is stretched out with a beer in one hand and bread and sausage in the other. He lies facing the water, watching two children, other people's children, playing on the beach below. He doesn't hear Beth because he is concentrating on the children.

They must be brother and sister, George decides. Their pails and shovels have been abandoned at the water's edge, and they are overturning rocks to expose the little crabs that hide beneath them. With each rock that is overturned, they shriek and recoil in ecstatic horror as the crabs scramble frantically for new cover. The little boy reaches out gingerly with a sneakered toe and nudges one or two of the crabs that have stopped moving. The little girl hovers warily behind him.

George smiles, watching. Maybe later he will go down and show them that the crabs can be picked up, so, holding them by the shell so that the pincers are at a safe distance.

2.

Beth has found pen and paper and is making lists. She notes the details from one brochure and compares them with another. She has a second piece of paper for groceries. The cabin was stocked when they arrived, but you never know what you might need. She has also noted a few spider webs that need to be cleaned away, and she should really get a few postcards in the mail if she is going to town for groceries. She looks at George, just lying there, and thinks that she had better get on with it. You can just tell by looking that *he* isn't going to be any help.

3.

Below them, on the beach, the children are becoming braver. George watches as the two sunbleached, tousled heads merge over a rock. Together they heave against its barnacled surface until a new mess of crabs skitters across the beach. This time the boy puts his hand down on the sand, and George isn't sure if he means to pick up a crab or if he merely wants to see how close he can get. In any case, the crab veers away. The little girl's face is filled with admiration at her brother's bravery, and you can tell she is itching to try it, too.

4.

George peels himself from the lounge chair and goes to the fridge for another beer. "Seeing as how you're up, could you hold this for me?" Beth asks, waving a pail and cloth at him. She has a chair pulled next to the window and wants to clean some bird poop from the top corner. George holds the pail, but his eyes are on the beach, on the children.

The little girl is crouched, elbows on knees and hair falling over her face, peering at the side of a rock. Her skin is sunbronzed and peeling, and she reaches back absently to scratch behind an ear. She is about four years old, George guesses. The boy, who is a bit older, has gone to the water to collect his pail, and on the way back he picks up a stick. They have a great discussion when he returns, with a good deal of pointing and gesturing. There must be a hole under the rock, George thinks, and they are going to poke into it.

5.

"There!" says Beth, giving the cloth a final rinse. "You couldn't see a thing out of that window." She relieves George of the pail and empties it into the sink.

George takes his chair and his beer outside. The sun is higher now, and shimmers gently on the water. The Gulf Islands are hazy in the distance, and a few sails are visible on the horizon. He moves out onto the sand, closer to the children. Nearby, two seagulls fight over a piece of garbage, their squabbling drowning out what the children are saying. George picks up a piece of driftwood and flings it at the birds, and they fly off, complaining.

The children's voices float up to him.

"It went in there," says the girl, pointing under the rock. They peer, cautious, faces close to the ground. Suddenly they grab the stick, and together they poke it under the rock, again and again, jabbing with increasing violence. Then they back off and wait.

6.

Behind him, in the cabin, Beth is finishing up the cupboards. She knows this is a holiday, but you have to stay organized. It's no fun running out of things just because the cupboards are in such disarray that you don't even know what's in stock. She glances at her watch and thinks she probably has time to wash her hair before they go into town for supplies. She sees George doing absolutely nothing out there in his chair, and irritation prickles her so that she has to fight the impulse to call out to him, to rouse him from what looks to her like a sheer waste of time. For the briefest of moments, she feels a bit envious. She knows she could never be like that, so relaxed, so free of care, not careless exactly, but able to enjoy this moment without worrying about later.

7.

A breeze sweeps across the sand and the water, and the sails are fuller now, the waves are growing higher. The little girl's hair is blown back from her face, and the wind carries her words down the beach, but George can tell by her expression that she is talking with a great deal of excitement. The children have moved forward, back to the rock, side by side, still cautious, still holding the stick between them. They reach out with it and nudge something gingerly and wait. Apparently nothing happens, and they reach out again with the stick, more boldly this time. Then the little girl lets go and stoops to pick up the red plastic pail, which she lays flat on the sand like a dustpan. Her brother scrapes and pushes until a mixture of sand and rocks and a large green crab, motionless, is deposited in the pail. They stare at it, heads touching over the red rim. Then they run to the sea, each with one hand on the handle of the pail, to add enough water to cover the dead crab. And, walking very carefully with the pail between them, they head down the beach to one of the other cabins.

8.

George watches until they are out of sight. He wonders what's keeping Beth. He turns and sees that the curtains have been pulled across the window of their cabin, and he remembers, now, her saying that she wanted to go somewhere. Supplies, he thinks it was. He snuggles deeper into his chair, taking comfort from her ability to take charge, to make sure all the details are worked out.

Soon he hears the car start, and Beth pokes her head around the corner.

"Are you coming?" she calls out. "I'm all ready to go."

"Coming," he replies, indulgently, folding up his chair. And they leave for the store, the grocery list between them.

Claudia Stewart

Prince Rupert writer and artist Claudia Stewart illustrated Joan Skogan's *Grey Cat at Sea* and *Princess and the Sea Bear* (Polestar Press). She has been writing a weekly arts and entertainment column for *Prince Rupert This Week* for over three years, and is involved in the local theatre group, Harbour Theatre.

"Angels" was written as a Christmas gift for the author's daughter and mother. It first appeared in the Sunday, Dec. 15, 1991 issue of *Prince Rupert This Week.*

All my Christmases are connected, strung together in my mind like popcorn or cranberries. The string that holds them is the sharing, the love, and some traditions.

I recall my mother getting down the big Christmas box from the attic each year. I was always a little bit scared when she came down the ladder, because the box was so huge, and the climb down the ladder so precarious. Both my sister and I hung onto the ladder to steady it. That box had all kinds of decorations in it; the blonde-haired angel with an iridescent white robe for the top of the tree, twinkle lights, glass balls (which I was given strict instructions not to touch, but did anyway) and some ornaments made by us kids.

My favourite was a little gingerbread man of brown construction paper that my sister had made. I thought I would never be coordinated or talented enough to make something like that. It had round paper buttons pasted on; purple and orange and green. It had blue eyes and a crooked red smile. I loved it.

Then I was in kindergarten, and we made red and green paper chains. Mine got mixed up and I put two greens beside each other, but my mother said she was proud of me and that it was a great chain. She hung it at the front of the tree, right in the middle.

A few years later, I made another tree decoration from two of those little cardboard cups from an egg carton. I glued them together and painted green and red stripes on my creation. The red stripes dribbled into the green a bit, but my mother said it looked more decorative that way, and hung that next to my big sister's gingerbread man.

We cut snowflakes one year. Went crazy with them, folding squares of paper into quarters, then into thirds, snipping out the frozen spokes of the flakes, making lacy holes. The living room rug looked as if it had been covered in snow.

It took me a long time to make anything that even resembled a snowflake and it looked like it would've hit the ground with a wet slap. But my mum hung it on the front of the tree with my sister's perfect spider-web one and said it was beautiful.

Every year our family would make something for Christmas. One year when my mother was Campfire Girl leader we all made candleholders. We broke bottles and glued the broken glass onto inexpensive water goblets, then put grout in the spaces between and rubbed the grout with lampblack so it looked like stained glass. Tempers got a bit short, but that year our family ate Christmas dinner by the light of that candle. Red and green and amber light danced across the mashed potatoes and made the cranberry sauce look like a river of molten lava.

Last Christmas when I got down the big box of ornaments from the attic, my daughter stood at the bottom of the ladder.

"Careful, Mum," Veronika called helpfully, standing right at the bottom rung.

"Look out, please, I'm about to tip over," I replied, trying to get a better grip on the heavy container.

When we had taken everything out, and gotten right to the bottom of the box, I remembered we had thrown out the cheap aluminium star last Christmas.

"Darn," I said. "We'll have to go down to the drugstore and pick up another."

"Let's have an angel, Mum," said my daughter. So I agreed and left her to do some colouring in the middle of the living room floor.

When she asked for the scissors, I got down off the chair from hanging a paper chain and gave them to her. When she asked for the tape, I said, through a mouthful of pins, "Top drawer of the desk," and continued pinning Christmas cards to a piece of red ribbon, while her dad and miscellaneous male friends and relatives strung the lights on the tree.

She grumbled at the tape and I asked if I could help, but she said that no, it was a surprise. When she was finished, she showed us.

The angel had brown hair and an awkward smile. Her dress was filled with hearts and flowers of different colours, a purple rabbit, and a yellow duck. Her purple wings were curved triangles and her arms were orange. There were actually two angels. Both smiled thick lipstick smiles, pink on one side, orange on the other. Both were taped at the top and on the sides, and open at the bottom so she/they could fit over the top of the tree.

"I messed up a bit on the tape," said Veronika doubtfully.

"It's the most beautiful angel I've ever seen," I replied.

We all smiled and bent the tree over and put Veronika's angel right on the top.

Liz McKenna

Dear Abby:

I have read your column for years, but have never written to you before. I don't have a marital problem, but have trouble with my children stealing my baking supplies.

We live quite a ways out of town so I buy lots of groceries when I do shop, especially raisins, dates and shredded coconut. I get mad when I go to the cupboard and find that I don't have enough ingredients to bake a cake. I've asked my five children who is eating them. None of them will admit to it. I cannot punish all five for something which maybe only one is doing. What do you suggest?

(Signed)   Frustrated

Dear Frustrated:

Thank you for writing. The only suggestion I can offer is that you put a lock on your cupboard door, and wear the key around your neck at all times.

(Signed)   Abby

Dear Abby:

Maybe you remember that I wrote to you about my children stealing my baking supplies. Your suggestion worked. It was a bit strange always having to take the key off my neck, unlock the cupboard, get my supplies out, then replace it, but I soon got used to this.

Unfortunately, I didn't lock the dried prunes in this cupboard. My husband likes stewed prunes every morning for breakfast. Now they are disappearing.

Until now, the children wouldn't look at prunes. I cannot see how they can be missing anything in their diet. I serve them good, wholesome food. Anyway, I'd really like to find out if it's one or all of the children who is stealing them.

(Signed)   At Wit's End

Dear At Wit's End:

I think I can help you with the prune problem. Why don't you take the pits out of the prunes and substitute some black pepper?

(Signed)   Abby

Dear Abby:

Regarding your advice about the prunes. I found the culprit. It was my husband. He was very upset. Now he is talking divorce, and I now sure as hell have a marital problem. What should I do?

(Signed)   Broken Hearted

Dear Broken Hearted:

That's the pits.

(Signed)   Abby

Marylou Fritch

"Axeman" was inspired by people's comments about odd people who tend to go to remote areas, away from the general population.

When school started up again in September, the children had a new bogy-man. Over the summer, their tales of *Dashina*, a local sasquatch legend, had been supplanted by something they called "Axeman." Anywhere else, we would have paid little attention, assuming that this was some character from the latest blood-curdling horror film. But, this small outpost was isolated from such 20th century commonplaces as telephones, and television and radio stations. Even movies were rare, and we knew full well that the few the children saw were out-of-date and innocuous.

At any rate, "Axeman" was to be taken seriously; so we questioned the children about him. They assured us that he was a very scary man who lived out of town and who carried an axe wherever he went. He was reputed to use his axe for killing (and, presumably, eating) dogs. The children could name several dogs thought to have met their end this way. They also expressed the conviction that he might use his axe in a similar manner on children, should they happen to cross his path.

A few questions to adults in town revealed that such a man did exist and that he did indeed carry an axe with him, though the dog killing was generally thought to be apocryphal. (At least one of the missing dogs had been dispatched by its owner, after stealing some meat intended for dinner.) He was certainly very strange and quite likely crazy enough to be an escapee from a mental institution, but probably harmless. He had shown up one day in early July and had built himself a shack of sorts by the river, about eight miles from town. Occasionally someone driving out that way saw him on the road and once every couple of weeks he showed up in town and bought some flour, sugar, and tea.

He was just the latest in a long line of crazy men who had wandered to this edge of a society they could not fit into. Many of us considered ourselves to be misfits too. We were in this remote place precisely because it appeared to be well outside of modern times. Most people in town expressed some empathy for this lonely man and his desire to be left alone.

One day, shortly after Labour Day, I saw him on his way out of town. He was that indeterminate late middle age that could be forty-five or sixty-five, a tall, gaunt figure with matted hair and feral eyes. I may have felt sympathy for him when speculating about his history with my neighbours, but the sight of Axeman striding along, muttering to himself, with an axe clearly protruding from his homemade pack, left me wondering if I should start locking my door at night. Axeman was pretty intimidating, and it was easy to see why the children had made him the stuff of nightmares.

As time passed, he came to town less and less often. I suppose whatever money he had arrived with was quickly used up and he must have had to increasingly rely on what he could catch or kill. Busy with our lives, we didn't really think of him very often. Even the children stopped chasing each other in his name and returned to more traditional monsters. Frank, who drove a grader for Highways, did walk down to check up on him one afternoon when he hadn't been seen in town for nearly a month. Axeman was home all right; he chased Frank back up to the road with curses. After that, people were just as glad that, if he was out of sight, he could also be out of mind.

In the North, the end of summer begins when the first "termination dust" shows up on the mountains in mid-August. By the middle of September, fall arrives with sudden splendour. The trees outshine the sun, and we are intoxicated with the scent of highbush cranberry as we walk along the hillside. The first of October usually finds little to remind us of those days. Now comes the "grey time": grey trees stand silhouetted against a grey sky, chocolate brown mud solidifies into an endless expanse of grey frozen dirt, and even the deep blue lake takes on a leaden cast. Over the years, I had come to appreciate the "grey time" as a sort of purgatory. It prepared my spirit to welcome the six months of winter with the joy appropriate to paradise, rather than with the dread and foreboding I felt when that first hint of chill insinuated itself into a sunny August afternoon.

As a rule, the "grey time" ended about Halloween with six inches or so of snow. Through the next two months, the snowpack would build by three-inch increments and the mean temperature would gradually drop. By Christmas, we would be safely ensconced in our snug homes, mentally and physically prepared for the snowstorms and -40 temperatures that usually accompanied the New Year.

This year, however, the weather stayed unusually mild well into November. Thanksgiving weekend we went for a picnic, to enjoy the prolonged show of leaves. I thought briefly of Axeman when I suggested that we go up the lake rather than down the river for our outing. A week later, a heavy rainfall inaugurated the "grey time," but the temperatures continued mild enough that we had to contend with mud, rather than snow, when our kids went trick-or-treating.

The long weekend in November was still quite mild. Monday afternoon the wind shifted to the north and it felt colder. By Tuesday morning, it had shifted again and brought a storm in from the coast. This time, snow fell. Twenty hours later, it shifted back to the north again, and we began digging out from a surprising fourteen-inch dump. Immediately, the temperature plummeted to -30 and hardly rose the next day. People hurriedly moved their woodpiles nearer to the house and rooted around for those essential items unwisely left out in the yard. The temperatures remained at that unseasonably cold level for the remainder of the week.

In the bustle of keeping fires stoked, roads and driveways plowed, and locating winter clothing, no one thought about Axeman. Even if we had, the road down the river, with only the Camerons, the Goulds and a few others living on it, was always the last plowed. So it would not have been easy to travel out that way. Thursday night, the Highways equipment finally started working in that direction.

About 9:30 Friday morning, Joyce Cameron radioed in for a medevac for an injured person. The plow truck, with the RCMP following, plowed a single lane out to the Camerons' place at 22 Mile. By noon, the police had brought the fellow to the airstrip. From there he was flown out to the hospital in Prince George.

My friend Karen's husband, Dave, was the plow truck driver and he stayed for coffee and a gossip with Joyce Cameron before continuing that morning. Joyce told him that she was just serving up some oatmeal to the kids when she heard something at the front door. Lois, the eldest, opened the door and an exhausted old man stumbled into the room. He was pretty incoherent and clearly suffering from exposure. She and the kids got him into dry clothes and she kept pouring hot coffee into him until the RCMP arrived. Joyce told Dave that he hadn't made a lot of sense, but she thought the storm had caught him away from home and he had wandered through the snow until he found their place. When he started to thaw, his hands and feet had begun to hurt real bad. She was relieved when the RCMP got there.

At first there was some doubt as to who the injured man was, since sometime, during his ordeal, he had lost his pack and his signature axe. The consensus was, finally, that it must have been Axeman. Certainly, Axeman was never seen again.

One Saturday in June, we went looking for Axeman's camp. The way down to the river was pretty obvious, but the high water in May must have washed the shack away. We couldn't find a trace. A trucker coming through told Jenny down at the cafe that he had heard they had to amputate both of Axeman's feet. But someone else, who had a cousin in Prince George, said it was just a few toes and a finger.

Mallory Burton

Mallory Burton has a serious fishing habit. During the winter, she teaches English as a Second Language and fishes for salmon and steelhead. Every summer, she makes a pilgrimage to Montana to thaw out, fish using tiny dry flies, and write fiction. Her work appears in flyfishing magazines and anthologies.

"Messing with the River Gods" was inspired by a fishing experience. It was previously published in *Flyfishing* (November/December 1991).

Every season for the past ten seasons, you have made a faithful pilgrimage to this river of rivers. In all the years you have visited these waters, you have taken away with you only the memories of a few special fish. You have left behind only your footprints and perhaps a few flies in the willows. In the company of other anglers, you have referred to this stretch of water only as the River X.

You figure your fishing karma on this particular river must be pretty good. So why in the name of all the river gods is the ten o'clock trico hatch in full swing at nine-thirty in the morning? And why is another fisherman standing in the middle of your favorite run with a good fish bending his rod and better fish rising all around him?

Under these circumstances, a lesser angler might rudely cut in upstream and muddy up the bottom of the river real good. But not you. Fortunately, or unfortunately depending on how you look at it, your fishing manners are impeccable. You'd no more cut in upstream than you'd go fishing with a can of worms and a jar of cheese balls. It's not that you're a fanatic about stream etiquette. It's just that it doesn't pay to mess with the river gods.

You step into the water at a respectful distance downstream and watch as the gentleman lands his fish. He raises the net, revealing the big forked tail and greyish mottled sides of what is obviously the most disgusting whitefish in three counties. A smile creeps over your face. Slowly everything begins to make perfect sense. After all, if the river gods have seen fit to place another angler in your favorite fishing spot and transform that spot into whitefish heaven, who are you to question their motives? Trusting entirely in their wisdom, you tie on a size 20 trico and calmly shake out a few feet of line.

Something catches your eye on the bottom of the stream. Through the swirling water, you can clearly make out a huge red-orange lure, all three of its barbaric hooks grinning up at you. Your forehead wrinkles in disgust. The river gods will not be pleased. You feel it is somehow your duty to remove the offending object from their domain. On the other hand, the water is waist-deep and spring-creek cold. You'll take a bath if you reach for it.

Just then, a few feet off the right riverbank, something very curious happens which suddenly demands your full attention. In smooth, flat water, all of six inches deep, a small boulder suddenly appears and behind it, a riffle that fans out four feet wide and twenty feet long. As you watch, the boulder disappears, reappears, and eats a trico. You dare to hope that the riffle is, in fact, a raft of feeding fish lying tail to snout in the wake of the monster at their head.

You fire a perfect cast at the head fish, cursing your stupidity the instant the fly hits the water. If you hook or even spook the lead fish, the others will scatter. You hold your mouth just right, and the fish ignores your fly. The fish behind him goes for it and misses. The fly slides over the back of another fish and into the upper jaw of the next fish down the line. You set the hook and the fish comes obediently downstream, silvery pink sides flashing.

You decide to pick off the trout one by one, working through the fourteen-inchers at the back toward the monster at the front. You cast into the tail end of the pack. A fish turns and pursues the fly downstream, nearly colliding with another fish that streaks over to snatch it away. You land this fish, another saucy rainbow, and release him.

Then it happens. The upstream fisherman reels in, clambers up the bank, and starts walking toward you. He takes his time, stopping every few feet to peer over the side of the undercut right river bank. Panic-stricken, you gesture frantically, motioning the intruder away from the bank, away from your fish. The angler stops in his tracks, looking puzzled. Then he turns in the direction of your frenzied pointing and nods his head, finally comprehending.

"Grouse," he shouts, cupping his hands around his mouth so that the sound will carry even better. "A pair." And he keeps on coming.

For centuries, the rules of fishing etiquette have been modelled by esteemed mentors and publicized by concerned writers. Trouble is, there exists no effective means of enforcing them. If an angler chooses to walk downstream close to the bank, shouting, there is nothing to prevent him or her from doing so.

You find yourself wishing that every fishing vest came equipped with a hand grenade. No, not a hand grenade. That would be too noisy. What you really need is a bow and a single silent arrow, straight and true. Thwack. Toppling the intruder backwards. Away from the fish. You wonder whether the jurisdiction of the river gods extends above the high water mark.

The riffle disappears, dark shapes streaking past you on every side, and with them your dark thoughts. The madness passes, and the gentle angler within you returns to inhabit your waders. You remind yourself that the creature on the bank is a human being, while the creatures in the water are, after all, only stupid fish.

"Howdy," says the human being, smiling and oblivious. "Catchinany?"

"A few," you say. "But it looks like it's all over now."

"What about later?" he asks. "Boys at the shop said this river's got a noon hatch of mayflies."

You nod in agreement. "Some stretches are better than others," you say thoughtfully. "There's a decent stretch about four miles upstream. Turnoff is just after the bridge. Can't miss it."

The two of you hike back to where your cars are parked, chatting amiably. You take down your rod and offer him a beer. You give him a half-dozen of the sparkle duns you tied in the wee hours of last night.

"What do I owe you for the flies?" he asks.

"Tell you what," you say. "The next time you're on your home river, just give away a few flies, and we'll call it even."

"I'll do that," he says. "People sure are friendly around here."

As his pickup heads off down the road, you give him the thumbs up sign. Then you string up your rod again, faster than you thought humanly possible. On the way back down the trail, you make a bargain with the river gods. If they bring back the riffle fish, you will take a swim in the icy river to retrieve the treble-hooked lure that is currently polluting their aquatic environment.

The river gods keep their end of the bargain. By the time you have hiked back down the trail, mayflies are popping all over the place, and the fish are back. You take twenty fish in twenty casts. The big rainbow goes four pounds easy.

You forget about your end of the bargain. Understandably, when you're having a day like the one you're having, you tend to get a little preoccupied. As you release the big trout and watch him swim away, you feel positively light-headed. You take a few steps toward the bank and trip over a boulder you're sure wasn't there this morning. As you go under, sputtering, you remember the lure. You mark its location with the toe of your boot, take a deep breath, and plunge into the icy water again and again. It's not that you're a fanatic about stream garbage. It's just that it doesn't pay to mess with the river gods.

N. J. Kerby

"Lottery" was inspired by some of the Northwest B.C.'s residents.

Anger that one small piece of paper
        random numbers random numbers
Did more to his life in five gaudy minutes
Than forty faithful years hardworking
                sweat   head down and dirty hands.
So what do you do with
Two million dollars
When your wife is bedridden
And the cancer in your lungs
Gnaws
Away the months?

Diamond Peter Charlie
Won five hundred thousand.
Spent one glorious drunken year
Surrounded by Drambuie bottles and darting sharks.
He sits in his cabin now,
Damn broke but happy.
Dat sure was one good party, he grins
Through the mansion
Of broken teeth.

for Jock McLean

Andrew Wreggitt

"Devilfish" was inspired by experiences on the North Coast.

You have to go right inside,
head first, right up to the beak
and hang on to those two
tentacles that aren't used for swimming
sixteen foot long
You have to shake 'em like a bugger
so he won't stop, just keep swimming
and not get the idea
of wrapping around you
He's scared too,
trying to run away
not ever thinking he could squeeze you in half
any time he wanted
600 pounds of him
flying through the water
and you're along for the ride

What you do then
is let him hold on to you
with the upper, webbed part of his tentacles
Makes a big bag with you
rammed in as a cork
Meanwhile the bubbles from the regulator
are fillin' him up like a big balloon
and you're headed for the surface
When you get there, you let go
and he spits you out

'cause he doesn't want nothing
to do with you in the first place
They're timid creatures despite the size
By then your partner in the boat's
got a gaff on him
and you're headin' for the Co-op

Anyway, that's how we done it in 1959
when octopus was 30 cents
 a pound

Richard Mackie

Richard Mackie is a freelance historian and biographer, with stories, poems, and reviews published in *The Beaver, Beautiful BC, Prairie Fire,* and *BC Studies.* He is author of *Hamilton Mack Laing: Hunter-Naturalist* (Sono Nis Press). A former Prince Rupert resident, he lives in Errington, Vancouver Island.

"Of course I am guilty of gross anthropomorphism, but the poem seemed to require it. The poem is about duty, predation, frustration, and Phillipa. I named her after an old girlfriend."

"You should see our boll weevils,"
said the doctoral candidate
from Nebraska
specializing in sexual predation:
"corn-fed and hand-spanked —
that's our State Motto."

Philippa the Octopus swims
just beyond Cougar Gap
under the boardwalk
in earthquake-inducing floodtide
unaware of these larger issues,
and blissfully ignorant
of theoretical constructs.
Instead she jumps on a sewer pipe
and fastens like a limpet,
slowly turning an oestral purple.

Philippa, I say through the rain,
this is 1989 not 1969.
Think of the threat of AIDS.
Think of the cult of frustration,
not to mention the vulgarity,

the shocking indecency
with which you wrap your legs tightly
(and at such close range too)
around that rusted pipe
like those dancers at the Globe Hotel,
Front Street, Nanaimo.

The tide, at least,
goes in and out,
day in and day out.

Gerry Deiter

Gerry Deiter was born in Brooklyn, New York. Once he and his wife discovered the B.C. coast, it was only a matter of time before they moved aboard a boat to explore the coastal wilderness, a pastime that occupies much of the Deiter family's time. His photography has appeared in *Life* and *Time*, and his writings in a variety of publications.

It's just a tiny dot in a small bay just off Seaforth Channel not far from Bella Bella . . . not much more than a rock sticking up from the deep waters of the cliff-faced inlet. But it marked a rite of passage for our son a couple of years ago.

We were on a summer cruise aboard our old cruiser *Luigi*, no destination really in mind; exploration and adventure were more what we were seeking.

The boy certainly was after adventure; just ten years old, he was beginning to outgrow his toy pirate boats, swords, books and fantasies . . . he was ready to start living them.

We'd been cruising all day, and as the purple June dusk deepened, we sought an anchorage for the night. We nosed into the little bay that looked so inviting on the chart, found a good anchoring ground, and dropped the hook. Immediately he wanted to go exploring, so as mom began dinner, we jumped into the Zodiac and buzzed off around the tiny bay.

He was fascinated by the little islet; he insisted we go ashore and explore it. It was only about 300 yards from the boat, and no more than about 50 feet in diameter at low tide, with a rocky shoreline broken by a narrow sandy strand that promised clams. As I hunted shellfish, he hunted pirates, stealthily moving between the scrubby trees and the brush above the high-tide line.

I called to him that it was getting near dinner time; he came back through the bushes with the determined look on his face that meant he'd had an idea he was going to sell me.

"Dad, would it be all right if I spent the night on this island? I could pitch my tent, build a fire, and I'd be all right . . . really. Please? PLEASE?"

We'd done some camping together, but sleeping in a tent is something I've never really enjoyed after being in the army. I replied that I really didn't feel like it; my bunk was far more comfortable.

"No, Dad," he replied impatiently. "Not us . . . ME!"

I thought long and hard about it; I didn't see any problem.

"Okay," I said. "We'll go back to the boat and get your gear."

Dinner was just about on the table when we returned.

"No dinner for me, Mom," he announced. "I'm going to cook my own over a campfire on that little island over there. Dad said I could."

I'd intended to break this bit of news to his mother with a bit more subtlety.

"Just what do you think you two are doing?" she demanded.

"Well, he said he'd like to camp on that little island for the night and I don't really think it's a bad idea . . . what about you?" ("We'd have the boat all to ourselves," I added seductively, "and you know there's a full moon tonight.")

It was as though we'd suggested he join the U.S. Marines.

"What, sleep out there by himself? What about the bears and the wolves?"

While I was assuring her there was very little chance he'd be devoured by a foraging carnivore on the little island, he simply ignored her maternal concerns and started hauling out his gear.

First came the tent, then the sleeping bag, ground pad, hatchet, knife, three flashlights, first aid kit, cooking kit and utensils. Then the fire starter and lighter, emergency ration pack (candy bars, Japanese noodle soup he loved to eat raw, cookies, Kraft dinner, sugared cereal, restaurant portions of jams, jellies and honey) . . . then he headed for the galley for his provisions.

His mother just stood there, stunned, watching the furious activity as I helped him load his gear into the Zodiac.

"I'll want you to take the hand-held VHF — we'll monitor channel 09 in case you have to call us — and a couple of flares, just in case," I told him.

"How about the rifle, Dad?" he inquired hopefully; then seeing my expression, decided not to press the question.

"You guys are really serious about this, aren't you?" Mom demanded.

"Of course," we answered in unison.

"And you're not going to listen to anything I have to say?"

"Sure we'll listen," he responded, "just so long as you don't say I can't go."

She looked at me.

"Don't worry," I assured her. "He'll be all right."

"Oh, sure . . . wolves, bears, snakes."

"And pirates, Mom . . . don't forget the pirates."

"You've made up your mind?"

"Do you want to tell him no?"

At this point, she retreated to the galley muttering about ruined dinner, no sleep tonight, what a pair of fools we both were.

The Zodiac was so loaded it wouldn't even plane, but we beached and unloaded it and I offered to help him get set up. He wouldn't hear of it.

"You go back to Mom," he insisted. "I can do everything myself."

I insisted on helping him pitch the tent and lay the fire. As we finished, he decided a ceremony was in order, and took possession of the islet in the name of our family.

"We'll call it Family Isle," he announced.

I left him some final instructions, then pushed off and covered the distance to the boat in a few seconds. His mother was still fretting.

"Come on; let's have a drink," I urged, and managed to get her to relax a bit.

I had in the meanwhile checked the tide table again; it was the solstice and a full moon; the tidefall was pretty big. I estimated how high it would come on the tiny beach; I had a moment of anxiety in which I almost wished I hadn't made the decision to let him stay, but it was too late now. But most of all, I had to make sure his mother didn't sense any concern on my part.

As darkness fell, we finished dinner and stood on deck watching the huge yellow moon sprinkle silver highlights on the water. His campfire glowed, spitting out occasional sparks, and we could hear him across the water, bustling about, singing and talking to himself.

I called him on the radio at about 11 p.m., reminding him it was time to douse the fire and go to sleep; he replied he was banking the fire, Dad, so he could raise it in the morning to cook his breakfast, and yes, he was going to bed.

We did too, but I couldn't sleep . . . I kept thinking about that rising tide that was to be high at about 2 a.m. At about 1 a.m., ensuring my wife was asleep, I got up and put the binoculars on the island. His fire, built only a few feet from the tent flap, was just glowing; I was reassured the water hadn't risen that high . . . yet. I whispered into the radio to see if he'd answer . . . he was asleep. I turned on the boat's small searchlight and painted the island with its beam. I was horrified to see how little was left above water, and it was still an hour from high tide on the table.

That did it . . . no sleep for me. I climbed into my clothes and quietly slipped the Zodiac's painter. I made it a point to row the skiff. . . . I was going to awaken no one unless absolutely necessary. I beached it quietly near his tent, crept near to ensure everything was all right. He was sleeping like a baby. The water was about six feet from the embers of his campfire and still rising. I estimated it wouldn't go much further, but I was taking no chances. No sleep tonight . . . I was staying until the tide turned.

I fought my sleepiness as I rocked to and fro in the little rubber boat, turning on my flashlight every few minutes to check my watch and the height of the water on the beach, wishing I was back in my bunk. Finally, after a little more than an hour, I was satisfied the tide had turned and quietly rowed back to *Luigi*, the oars swirling phosphorescent whirlpools, the wake a shimmering green trail in the water.

We were awakened early the next morning by a cheery call on the VHF. He told us how wonderfully he'd slept, how he'd managed to re-start his campfire from the embers he'd banked, and was cooking breakfast; then he suggested he stay the rest of the day and the next night.

I finally had to use my veto power . . . I just couldn't take another night of his self-sufficiency.

N. J. Kerby

I had forgotten   what love is like

    a simple ceremony at Heritage Park
    a few friends   his two kids kicking
    piles of dust with pointed shoes
    almost embarrassed   sarcastic jokes
    her second   groom's third
why don't they just live together, someone says

but I had forgotten   what love is like
    until they kissed
    and in that moment
    the passion of their promises
    bright with daisy chains and
    blown into the summer winds
until that moment   I had forgotten
        to them
        it did not matter

Pat Barry

Former Prince Rupert resident Pat Barry graduated from the University of Victoria with a BFA in theatre and creative writing in 1984. She has done copywriting for a variety of northwestern B.C. companies.

"You're not going to cry, are you?" my mother asked, stuffing extra handkerchiefs into her bag.

I leaned against the back wall of the church and watched my relatives engage in handshakes and cheek kissing with all the efficiency of an assembly line. My aunt presided over the whole thing like she was hostessing one of her cosmetic parties. There was even a guest book to sign.

"Why St. Patrick's?" my sister whispered to my mother. "She never came here."

"Your aunt thought it was more convenient," I heard my mother reply.

A battalion of little old men and women surged past me, filling the back rows of the church. A few straggled down to the front to light candles and pray.

*　　*　　*

I remember Nana. I remember lying next to her in the creaky, mahogany bed, listening to her recite the rosary. Each word of each prayer spoken like an incantation between short puffs of whiskey breath. She was eighty. Whiskey and religion filled her days, beginning and ending them in a slow kind of pattern.

"Nana? What happens when you die?"

"You go to Heaven."

"What happens if you go to HELL?" How I liked the sound of that word, especially the way Father Stuart said it. He could take a word with one syllable and stretch it into three.

"I don't know much about Hell, Frannie. I'm not planning to go there."

So she told me about Heaven instead. The way she described the angels, the harp music, and living inside the clouds reminded me of an ice cream sundae with mounds of whipping cream on top. I thought in terms of food when I was five.

"But if you live forever in Heaven, how come you have to die?"

"So that you can live forever with God."

"Dying's sad. Everyone cried when Bambi's mother died. I don't want to die!"

"Dying doesn't have to be sad, Frannie. People make it that way and sometimes they cry for the wrong reasons." She sighed and pulled me closer. She smelled of Devon violets. Sometimes in her bathroom, I would baptize myself in Devon violets and reek of it for days.

*   *   *

"The grace of our Lord, Jesus Christ, and the fellowship of the Holy Spirit be with you all."

My mind on automatic pilot, I answered the responsorial psalm. My eyes focused on the coffin in front. The flowers swaying like a mountain on top. Her rosary beads resting gently on top of the floral spray like a flag draped over a soldier's casket.

My voice came from far away. It was breathy, shaky, and not mine. My mother, mistaking the quiver in my voice for sorrow, laid her hand over mine. Abruptly I moved away.

"Lord bless our sister, Mary Frances. lying before us in her imperfect state. Forgive, Oh Lord, her sins and bring her forward into salvation."

What sins had a ninety-three-year-old woman committed? I heard the sounds of rosary beads clacking against the back of a pew and what I imagined were the soft mutterings of an old woman.

*   *   *

I was four the first time Nana took me to the cathedral. Our footsteps echoed on the marble floor. We lit candles and then Nana took me around the stations of the cross. We stopped and prayed at each one of the pictures. Christ being stripped. Christ being dragged through the streets. Christ being nailed to the cross. God was everywhere. God was in the pews. God was in the candle grease and the stained glass windows looking down on me. God was watching me. God was listening to my thoughts, and Nana, as if anticipating all this, turned to me and said, "Be careful what you think."

My religious years began. I was communionized, confirmed, and confessed. Nana gave me a little gold cross.

Every Sunday she would take me to mass. The church was as cold and sterile as the marble it was built upon, and Father Stuart as cold and unappetizing as the prunes Nana fed me for breakfast. He would roll his eyes towards the ceiling so quickly that I thought his eyes were on ball bearings. Nana said he did this out of piety. Daddy said it was because the choir was off key.

Nana would take me by the hand and lead me down the communion line. The closer I got to Father Stuart, the more fiercely I'd pull on her hand. It never did any good. Father Stuart would place the host between Nana's lips, and I would look up and see the whites of his eyes, as large and luminous as ping pong balls, being devoured by his forehead.

*   *   *

"The body of Christ." The eyes of the young priest were soft and suffering. "Amen," I murmured, taking the host and placing it in my mouth. It tasted as it did then, dry and sour, disintegrating slowly. Closing my eyes, I tried hard to compose a prayer, but nothing came to me but the shuffling of feet and clearing of throats.

The priest lit incense in the censer and swung it over the coffin in a wide arc. The sweet sickly smell of incense billowed out and rose to the ceiling. The priest closed his eyes and soundlessly mouthed the words of a prayer. I pursed my lips and whispered softly. "Hocus. Pocus."

There was no mud at the cemetery, only the dry November leaves which crunched beneath our feet. We stood on the grass, high in the Catholic section, reciting the Lord's prayer. When this was finished, my aunt turned to me and said, "Poor soul. At least she'll have a nice view here."

Oceanview. Riverview. Mountainview. What did it matter what you looked out on. You were dead. How would you know what you looked out on? My grandmother was ten feet away from a bright green tarpaulin covering a mound of fresh dirt and gravedigger's equipment. Some view.

Why had people chosen this moment to cry? This moment was not particularly sad. This moment was quite silly when you thought about it. My aunt dabbed at her eyes. My sister turned away. My mother stood with her head bowed while Father gave a good resounding blow into his hanky. Old women were openly weeping. I remembered what my grandmother said a long time ago about people crying for the wrong reasons.

The priest made the sign of the cross over the coffin, then, bending down, removed the rosary beads from the flowers. It passed from hand to hand down the line of mourners . . . from my father's hands to my mother's, from my mother's hands to my sister's, from my sister's hands to my aunt's where it stopped one short of me.

She hadn't left much. No will. She hadn't much to give. She had died in a nursing home. On her nightstand was a photograph taken of her graduation from nursing school in 1915, a Bible, and her rosary beads. The obituary notice in the paper recorded the rest: Nine grandchildren. Eleven great grandchildren. The accomplishments of her life.

The rosary beads rattled in the November wind. My aunt clutched them tighter to stifle their sound. Poor soul, I thought. Not much of a keepsake. I have a much better one. One that would last me a lifetime. I have my grandmother's middle name.

Dorothy Trail Spiller

The ideas for "The Redeemer" came to Dorothy Trail Spiller while she was walking on her beach.

Tell your painful thoughts to the wind.
Riffles across the waves
fall into the sky
clean, cold as the green water.

Do not tell your thoughts to the woman
who walks on the beach
she has her own sharp knives
or the child on the street
who is centred in his own important self. Especially not to the
man you met in the Legion who orders you a single malt
but does not want to buy your thoughts.
He will listen with an abstracted air
impatient to tell you his own.
Your pain will still be within you
entangled in confusion of Eros and agape
to smother tenderness
to strangle love.

when tomorrow comes let your thoughts go.
Let them escape on the billowing wind,
redeemed for peace.
You will be empty.

Now wait once more to be filled.

Mallory Burton

"The Emerger" refers to hatching insects which flyfishers call "emergers," and to the author's son's emerging awareness of the catch and release ethic. This story has been previously published in *Flyfishing News, Views*, and *Reviews; Uncommon Waters: Women Write about Fishing* (Seal Press), and is to appear in *Outdoor Canadian Angler*.

Several years ago, at the beginning of fishing season, I bought my eight-year-old son a light-action spinning rod and reel.

"Mum," said Anthony as we drove away from the tackle shop, "is this really my very own fishing rod?"

"Of course it's your rod," I said, irritated that he would ask. I was a confirmed flyfisher and hadn't touched a spinning rod since before he was born.

I hoped, of course, that my son would eventually develop an interest in flyfishing, but I wasn't going to push him. Flyfishing isn't like that. Either it calls you or it doesn't.

We fished many of the lakes and rivers between Prince Rupert and Terrace that season, from tiny Lost Lake with its doubtful rowboats to the fast-flowing Copper River. Anthony fished with worms and briny-smelling gobs of salmon roe while I persisted in trying to raise trout to a floating fly.

Anthony enviously admired the stringers of cutthroat and Dolly Varden taken by the bait fishermen we encountered on rivers and lakeshores. He had almost given up trying to persuade me to keep the fish I caught, watching incredulous as I removed the barbless hooks and slipped the fish back into the water.

"But that's a keeper," he'd protest. "Why do you have to put him back?"

Because he took the fly so deliberately. Because he was a wild trout, not a hatchery fish. Because the exhausted fish came to my feet so quietly with none of the panicked, thrashing resistance that might have sparked some killing instinct in me. They were not the kinds of reasons that would have made sense to an eight-year-old.

Occasionally, I took pictures of the fish I released, especially the dark-spotted cutthroats with their scarlet slashes below their gill covers or the sleek, bright steelhead trout. Anthony kept all of his regulation-size fish. We had an agreement that I would fish for picture fish while he fished for food fish.

Fortunately, the wild stocks were in no danger from my fish-killing son, who wasn't patient enough to be very deadly. His tolerance was limited to one netted fish, one lost lure, or one hopelessly-tangled line, whichever came first. After that, he was content to build luxurious toad habitats or holding ponds where he watched his captured sculpins swim until they found a hole between the rocks and darted away.

He was particularly interested in collecting caddis larvae or dragonfly nymphs, which he put into plastic bug boxes and scrutinized with a cracked magnifying glass. Once he waded into the Lakelse River during a mayfly hatch to observe the worm-like nymphs floating up from the bottom of the river, emerging as winged adults on the surface. Together we watched the newly hatched adults drift across the surface to dry their wings for a few seconds before coming off the water. Later he sat beside me for hours as I tied nymph, emerger, and adult insect imitations on small hooks, advising me on their correct size and colour for the waters we were fishing. Eventually he fished with a fly I had tied.

After the Kloiya River closed for the season, I lost interest in fishing, but Anthony was still keen on fishing the lakes. Near the end of August he decided to try his luck at a pair of tiny lakes outside Prince Rupert which were really better suited for picnicking than angling. There might have been some larger fish in their depths, but I secretly doubted that any really decent fish would live in lakes named Tweedledum and Tweedledee. Anthony fished while I picked berries nearby.

I could tell it was going to be a short expedition. Arriving on the marshy shore, Anthony promptly stepped into the bog, filling his gumboots with reeking slime. And he was rapidly using up his supply of worms, winging them right off the hook with vigorous casts or losing them to the minnows which boiled around his bobber like a school of miniature piranhas. He would have been prepared to call it a day when the worms ran out, except for several larger rings on the water's surface which suggested better fish. I set down my berry pail and quickly knotted a trailing leader of six inches to a thumbnail spinner. I tied on a fly called a Muddler Minnow and handed it to him. He looked dubiously at the fly set-up but recognized it as a sculpin imitation and clipped it on the swivel in place of the bobber. His ferocious cast plunked the spinner well on the other side of the rising fish. Reeling in rapidly, he tried to jerk the tackle clear of a clump of reeds as it came within four feet of the bank, but the spinner caught in the rushes. As Anthony tugged on the snagged spinner, the trailing fly flopped wildly on the surface. Suddenly a fourteen-inch trout sailed through the air, nailing the Muddler with an angry splash. The force of its impact freed the snagged spinner, and the fish was airborne a second time as Anthony horsed it out of the water onto the shore. The cutthroat was legal size and therefore a goner. I thought.

To my surprise Anthony picked up the fish, carefully removed the hook, and eased the trout gently back into the water. He watched it swim away and turned with an odd expression on his face.

"What an incredible fish! Did you see the way he hit that fly?" I nodded. "Do they always hit a floating fly like that?"

"They don't often sail through the air, but you usually see the take."

My son's hands trembled slightly as he picked up his rod and slowly reeled in the line. He took a deep breath and shook his head.

"Awesome," he said. I knew the feeling.

E. W. Gant

"Lunch" was inspired by the author's experiences in the Northwest.

If I look like a salty dog
keeping his feet in a raging sea
forced beyond his imaginings
to survive —
I am

If I look like a piece of meat
standing in the dock
forming a bend and spread defence
while casing out the exits —
I am

If I look like a sacrificed man
throwing a fly to effect an escape
while leaving the ass end
of his heart behind —
I am

If I look like a part-time poet
trying to eye life
through the mined gems
of his existence
then I guess —
I am

If I look like a one-mate rake
walking past the appetizers
of a hand to mouth existence
to ask you out to lunch —
I am